A BUSINESS ENGAGEMENT

BY
MERLINE LOVELACE

Published in Great Britain 2013
by Mills & Boon, an imprint of Harlequin (UK) Limited,
Eton House, 18-24 Paradise Road, Richmond, Surrey TW9 1SR

© Merline Lovelace 2013

ISBN: 978 0 263 90484 0
ebook ISBN: 978 1 472 00633 2

51-0913

Harlequin (UK) policy is to use papers that are natural, renewable and recyclable products and made from wood grown in sustainable forests. The logging and manufacturing processes conform to the legal environmental regulations of the country of origin.

Printed and bound in Spain
by Blackprint CPI, Barcelona

A career Air Force officer, **Merline Lovelace** served at bases all over the world. When she hung up her uniform for the last time she decided to combine her love of adventure with a flair for storytelling, basing many of her tales on her own experiences in uniform. Since then she's produced more than ninety action-packed sizzlers, many of which have made the *USA TODAY* and Waldenbooks bestseller lists. Over eleven million copies of her books are available in some thirty countries.

When she's not tied to her keyboard, Merline enjoys reading, chasing little white balls around the fairways of Oklahoma and traveling to new and exotic locales with her handsome husband, Al. Check her website at www.merlinelovelace.com or friend her on Facebook for news and information about her latest releases.

To Susan and Monroe and Debbie and Scott and
most especially, le beau Monsieur Al.
Thanks for those magical days in Paris. Next time,
I promise not to break a foot—or anything else!

Prologue

Ah, the joys of having two such beautiful, loving granddaughters. And the worries! Eugenia, my joyful Eugenia, is like a playful kitten. She gets into such mischief but always seems to land on her feet. It's Sarah I worry about. So quiet, so elegant and so determined to shoulder the burdens of our small family. She's only two years older than her sister but has been Eugenia's champion and protector since the day those darling girls came to live with me.

Now Sarah worries about *me*. I admit to a touch of arthritis and have one annoying bout of angina, but she insists on fussing over me like a mother hen. I've told her repeatedly I won't have her putting her life on hold because of me, but she won't listen. It's time, I think, to take more direct action. I'm not quite certain at this point just what action, but something will come to me. It must.

From the diary of Charlotte,
Grand Duchess of Karlenburgh

One

Sarah heard the low buzz but didn't pay any attention to it. She was on deadline and only had until noon to finish the layout for *Beguile*'s feature on the best new ski resorts for the young and ultrastylish. She wanted to finish the mock-up in time for the senior staff's weekly working lunch. If she didn't have it ready, Alexis Danvers, the magazine's executive editor, would skewer her with one of the basilisk-like stares that had made her a legend in the world of glossy women's magazines.

Not that her boss's stony stares particularly bothered Sarah. They might put the rest of the staff in a flophouse sweat, but she and her sister had been raised by a grandmother who could reduce pompous officials or supercilious headwaiters to a quivering bundle of nerves with the lift of a single brow. Charlotte St. Sebastian had once moved in the same circles as Princess Grace and Jackie O. Those days were long gone, Sarah acknowledged, as she switched the headline font from Futura to Trajan, but Grandmama still adhered to the unshakable belief that good breeding and quiet elegance could see a woman through anything life might throw at her.

Sarah agreed completely. Which was one of the reasons she'd refined her own understated style during her three years as layout editor for a magazine aimed at thirtysome-things determined to be chic to the death. Her vintage Chanel suits and Dior gowns might come from Grandmama's closet, but she teamed the gowns with funky costume jewelry and the suit jackets with slacks or jeans and boots. The result was a stylishly retro look that even Alexis approved of.

The primary reason Sarah stuck to her own style, of course, was that she couldn't afford the designer shoes and bags and clothing featured in *Beguile*. Not with Grandmama's medical bills. Some of her hand-me-downs were starting to show their wear, though, and…

The buzz cut into her thoughts. Gaining volume, it rolled in her direction. Sarah was used to frequent choruses of oohs and aahs. Alexis often had models parade through the art and production departments to field test their hair or makeup or outfits on *Beguile*'s predominantly female staff.

Whatever was causing this chorus had to be special. Excitement crackled in the air like summer lightning. Wondering what new Jimmy Choo beaded boots or Atelier Versace gown was creating such a stir, Sarah swung her chair around. To her utter astonishment, she found herself looking up into the face of Sexy Single Number Three.

"Ms. St. Sebastian?"

The voice was cold, but the electric-blue eyes, black hair and rugged features telegraphed hot, hot, hot. Alexis had missed the mark with last month's issue, Sarah thought wildly. This man should have *topped* the magazine's annual Ten Sexiest Single Men in the World list instead of taking third place.

The artist in her could appreciate six-feet-plus of hard, muscled masculinity cloaked in the civilized veneer of a hand-tailored suit and Italian-silk tie. The professional in her responded to the coldness in his voice with equally cool civility.

"Yes?"

"I want to talk to you." Those devastating blue eyes cut to the side. "Alone."

Sarah followed his searing gaze. An entire gallery of female faces peered over, around and between the production department's chin-high partitions. A few of those faces were merely curious. Most appeared a half breath away from drooling.

She turned back to Number Three. Too bad his manners didn't live up to his looks. The aggressiveness in both his tone and his stance were irritating and uncalled for, to say the least.

"What do you want to talk to me about, Mr. Hunter?"

He didn't appear surprised that she knew his name. She did, after all, work at the magazine that had made hunky Devon Hunter the object of desire by a good portion of the female population at home and abroad.

"Your sister, Ms. St. Sebastian."

Oh, no! A sinking sensation hit Sarah in the pit of her stomach. What had Gina gotten into now?

Her glance slid to the silver-framed photo on the credenza beside her workstation. There was Sarah, dark-haired, green-eyed, serious as always, protective as always. And Gina. Blonde, bubbly, affectionate, completely irresponsible.

Two years younger than Sarah, Gina tended to change careers with the same dizzying frequency she tumbled in and out of love. She'd texted just a few days ago, gushing about the studly tycoon she'd hooked up with. Omitting, Gina style, to mention such minor details as his name or how they'd met.

Sarah had no trouble filling in the blanks now. Devon Hunter was founder and CEO of a Fortune 500 aerospace corporation headquartered in Los Angeles. Gina was in

L.A. chasing yet another career opportunity, this time as a party planner for the rich and famous.

"I think it best if we make this discussion private, Ms. St. Sebastian."

Resigned to the inevitable, Sarah nodded. Her sister's flings tended to be short and intense. Most ended amicably, but on several occasions Sarah had been forced to soothe some distinctly ruffled male feathers. This, apparently, was one of those occasions.

"Come with me, Mr. Hunter."

She led the way to a glass-walled conference room with angled windows that gave a view of Times Square. Framed prominently in one of the windows was the towering Condé Nast Building, the center of the universe for fashion publications. The building was home to *Vogue, Vanity Fair, Glamour* and *Allure.* Alexis often brought advertisers to the conference room to impress them with *Beguile*'s proximity to those icons in the world of women's glossies.

The caterers hadn't begun setting up for the working lunch yet but the conference room was always kept ready for visitors. The fridge discreetly hidden behind oak panels held a half-dozen varieties of bottled water, sparkling and plain, as well as juices and energy drinks. The gleaming silver coffee urns were replenished several times a day.

Sarah gestured to the urns on their marble counter. "Would you care for some coffee? Or some sparkling water, perhaps?"

"No. Thanks."

The curt reply decided her against inviting the man to sit. Crossing her arms, she leaned a hip against the conference table and assumed a look of polite inquiry.

"You wanted to talk about Gina?"

He took his time responding. Sarah refused to bristle as his killer blue eyes made an assessing trip from her face to her Chanel suit jacket with its black-and-white checks and signature logo to her black boots and back up again.

"You don't look much like your sister."

"No, I don't."

She was comfortable with her slender build and what her grandmother insisted were classic features, but she knew she didn't come close to Gina's stunning looks.

"My sister's the only beauty in the family."

Politeness dictated that he at least make a show of disputing the calm assertion. Instead, he delivered a completely unexpected bombshell.

"Is she also the only thief?"

Her arms dropped. Her jaw dropped with them. "I beg your pardon?"

"You can do more than beg my pardon, Ms. St. Sebastian. You can contact your sister and tell her to return the artifact she stole from my house."

The charge took Sarah's breath away. It came back on a hot rush. "How dare you make such a ridiculous, slanderous accusation?"

"It's neither ridiculous nor slanderous. It's fact."

"You're crazy!"

She was in full tigress mode now. Years of rushing to her younger sibling's defense spurred both fury and passion.

"Gina may be flighty and a little careless at times, but she would never take anything that didn't belong to her!"

Not intentionally, that is. There was that nasty little Pomeranian she'd brought home when she was eight or nine. She'd found it leashed to a sign outside a restaurant in one-hundred-degree heat and "rescued" it. And it was true Gina and her teenaged friends used to borrow clothes from each other constantly, then could never remember what belonged to whom. And, yes, she'd been known to overdraw her checking account when she was strapped for cash, which happened a little too frequently for Sarah's peace of mind.

But she would never commit theft, as this…this boor was suggesting. Sarah was about to call security to have the man escorted from the building when he reached into his suit pocket and palmed an iPhone.

"Maybe this clip from my home surveillance system will change your mind."

He tapped the screen, then angled it for Sarah to view. She saw a still image of what looked like a library or study, with the focus of the camera on an arrangement of glass shelves. The objects on the shelves were spaced and spotlighted for maximum dramatic effect. They appeared to be an eclectic mix. Sarah noted an African buffalo mask, a small cloisonné disk on a black lacquer stand and what looked like a statue of a pre-Columbian fertility goddess.

Hunter tapped the screen again and the still segued into a video. While Sarah watched, a tumble of platinum-blond curls came into view. Her heart began to thump painfully even before the owner of those curls moved toward the shelving. It picked up more speed when the owner showed her profile. That was her sister. Sarah couldn't even pretend to deny it.

Gina glanced over her shoulder, all casual nonchalance, all smiling innocence. When she moved out of view again, the cloisonné medallion no longer sat on its stand. Hunter froze the frame again, and Sarah stared at the empty stand as though it was a bad dream.

"It's Byzantine," he said drily. "Early twelfth century, in case you're interested. One very similar to it sold recently at Sotheby's in London for just over a hundred thousand."

She swallowed. Hard. "Dollars?"

"Pounds."

"Oh, God."

She'd rescued Gina from more scrapes than she could count. But this… She almost yanked out one of the chairs and collapsed in a boneless heap. The iron will she'd inherited from Grandmama kept her spine straight and her chin up.

"There's obviously a logical explanation for this, Mr. Hunter."

"I very much hope so, Ms. St. Sebastian."

She wanted to smack him. Calm, refined, always polite Sarah had to curl her hands into fists to keep from slapping that sneer off his too-handsome face.

He must have guessed her savagely suppressed urge. His jaw squared and his blue eyes took on a challenging glint, as if daring her to give it her best shot. When she didn't, he picked up where they'd left off.

"I'm very interested in hearing that explanation before I refer the matter to the police."

The police! Sarah felt a chill wash through her. Whatever predicament Gina had landed herself in suddenly assumed a very ominous tone. She struggled to keep the shock and worry out of her voice.

"Let me get in touch with my sister, Mr. Hunter. It may... it may take a while. She's not always prompt about returning calls or answering emails right away."

"Yeah, I found that out. I've been trying to reach her for several days."

He shot back a cuff and glanced at his watch.

"I've got meetings scheduled that will keep me tied up for the rest of this afternoon and well into the night. I'll make dinner reservations for tomorrow evening. Seven o'clock. Avery's, Upper West Side." He turned that hard blue gaze on her. "I assume you know the address. It's only a few blocks from the Dakota."

Still stunned by what she'd seen in the surveillance clip, Sarah almost missed his last comment. When it penetrated, her eyes widened in shock. "You know where I live?"

"Yes, Lady Sarah, I do." He tipped two fingers to his brow in a mock salute and strode for the door. "I'll see you tomorrow."

* * *

Lady Sarah.

Coming on top of everything else, the use of her empty title shouldn't have bothered her. Her boss trotted it out frequently at cocktail parties and business meetings. Sarah had stopped being embarrassed by Alexis's shameless peddling of a royal title that had long since ceased to have any relevance.

Unfortunately, Alexis wanted to do more than peddle the heritage associated with the St. Sebastian name. Sarah had threatened to quit—twice!—if her boss went ahead with the feature she wanted to on *Beguile*'s own Lady Sarah Elizabeth Marie-Adele St. Sebastian, granddaughter to Charlotte, the Destitute Duchess.

God! Sarah shuddered every time she remembered the slant Alexis had wanted to give the story. That destitute tag, as accurate as it was, would have shattered Grandmama's pride.

Having her younger granddaughter arrested for grand larceny wouldn't do a whole lot for it, either.

Jolted back to the issue at hand, Sarah rushed out of the conference room. She had to get hold of Gina. Find out if she'd really lifted that medallion. She was making a dash for her workstation when she saw her boss striding toward her.

"What's this I just heard?"

Alexis's deep, guttural smoker's rasp was always a shock to people meeting her for the first time. *Beguile*'s executive editor was paper-clip thin and always gorgeously dressed. But she would rather take her chances with cancer than quit smoking and risk ballooning up to a size four.

"Is it true?" she growled. "Devon Hunter was here?"

"Yes, he…"

"Why didn't you buzz me?"

"I didn't have time."

"What did he want? He's not going to sue us, is he?

Dammit, I told you to crop that locker-room shot above the waist."

"No, Alexis. You told me to make sure it showed his butt crack. And I told *you* I didn't think we should pay some smarmy gym employee to sneak pictures of the man without his knowledge or consent."

The executive editor waved that minor difference of editorial opinion aside. "So what did he want?"

"He's, uh, a friend of Gina's."

Or was, Sarah thought grimly, until the small matter of a twelfth-century medallion had come between them. She had to get to a phone. Had to call Gina.

"Another one of your sister's trophies?" Alexis asked sarcastically.

"I didn't have time to get all the details. Just that he's in town for some business meetings and wants to get together for dinner tomorrow."

The executive editor cocked her head. An all-too-familiar gleam entered her eyes, one that made Sarah swallow a groan. Pit bulls had nothing on Alexis when she locked her jaws on a story.

"We could do a follow-up," she said. "How making *Beguile*'s Top Ten list has impacted our sexy single's life. Hunter's pretty much a workaholic, isn't he?"

Frantic to get to the phone, Sarah gave a distracted nod. "That's how we portrayed him."

"I'm guessing he can't take a step now without tripping over a half-dozen panting females. Gina certainly smoked him out fast enough. I want details, Sarah. Details!"

She did her best to hide her agitation behind her usual calm facade. "Let me talk to my sister first. See what's going on."

"Do that. And get me details!"

Alexis strode off and Sarah barely reached the chair at her worktable before her knees gave out. She snatched up her iPhone and hit the speed-dial number for her sister. Of course, the call went to voice mail.

"Gina! I need to talk to you! Call me."

She also tapped out a text message and zinged off an email. None of which would do any good if her sister had forgotten to turn on her phone. Again. Knowing the odds of that were better than fifty-fifty, she tried Gina's current place of employment. She was put through to her sister's distinctly irate boss, who informed her that Gina hadn't shown up for work. Again.

"She called in yesterday morning. We'd catered a business dinner at the home of one our most important clients the night before. She said she was tired and was taking the day off. I haven't heard from her since."

Sarah had to ask. "Was that client Devon Hunter, by any chance?"

"Yes, it was. Look, Ms. St. Sebastian, your sister has a flair for presentation but she's completely unreliable. If you speak to her before I do, tell her not to bother coming in at all."

Despite the other, far more pressing problem that needed to be dealt with, Sarah hated that Gina had lost yet another job. She'd really seemed to enjoy this one.

"I'll tell her," she promised the irate supervisor. "And if she contacts you first, please tell her to call me."

She got through the working lunch somehow. Alexis, of course, demanded a laundry list of changes to the ski-resort layout. Drop shadows on the headline font. Less white space between the photos. Ascenders, not descenders, for the first letter of each lead paragraph.

Sarah made the fixes and shot the new layout from her computer to Alexis's for review. She then tried to frame another article describing the latest body-toning techniques. In between, she made repeated calls to Gina. They went unanswered, as did her emails and text messages.

Her concentration in shreds, she quit earlier than usual and hurried out into the April evening. A half block away, Times Square glowed in a rainbow of white, blue and brilliant-red lights. Tourists were out in full force, crowding the sidewalks and snapping pictures. Ordinarily Sarah took the subway to and from work, but a driving sense of urgency made her decide to splurge on a cab. Unbelievably, one cruised up just when she hit the curb. She slid in as soon as the previous passenger climbed out.

"The Dakota, please."

The turbaned driver nodded and gave her an assessing glance in the rearview mirror. Whatever their nationality, New York cabbies were every bit as savvy as any of *Beguile*'s fashion-conscious editors. This one might not get the label on Sarah's suit jacket exactly right but he knew quality when he saw it. He also knew a drop-off at one of New York City's most famous landmarks spelled big tips.

Usually. Sarah tried not to think how little of this month's check would be left after paying the utilities and maintenance fees for the seven-room apartment she shared with her grandmother. She also tried not to cringe when the cabbie scowled at the tip she gave him. Muttering something in his native language, he shoved his cab in gear.

Sarah hurried toward the entrance to the domed and turreted apartment building constructed in the 1880s and nodded to the doorman who stepped out of his niche to greet her.

"Good evening, Jerome."

"Good evening, Lady Sarah."

She'd long ago given up trying to get him to drop the empty title. Jerome felt it added to the luster of "his" building.

Not that the Dakota needed additional burnishing. Now a National Historic Landmark, its ornate exterior had been featured in dozens of films. Fictional characters in a host of novels claimed the Dakota as home. Real-life celebrities like Judy Garland, Lauren Bacall and Leonard Bernstein had lived there. And, sadly, John Lennon. He'd been shot just a short distance away. His widow, Yoko Ono, still owned several apartments in the building.

"The Duchess returned from her afternoon constitutional about an hour ago," Jerome volunteered. The merest hint of a shadow crossed his lean face. "She was leaning rather heavily on her cane."

Sharp, swift fear pushed aside Sarah's worry about her sister. "She didn't overdo it, did she?"

"She said not. But then, she wouldn't say otherwise, would she?"

"No," Sarah agreed in a hollow voice, "she wouldn't.

Charlotte St. Sebastian had witnessed the brutal execution of her husband and endured near-starvation before she'd escaped her war-ravaged country with her baby in her arms and a king's ransom in jewels hidden inside her daughter's teddy bear. She'd fled first to Vienna, then New York, where she'd slipped easily into the city's intellectual and social elite. The discreet, carefully timed sale of her jewels had allowed her to purchase an apartment at the Dakota and maintain a gracious lifestyle.

Tragedy struck again when she lost both her daughter and son-in-law in a boating accident. Sarah was just four and Gina still in diapers at the time. Not long after that, an unscrupulous Wall Street type sank the savings the duchess had managed to accrue into a Ponzi scheme that blew up in his and his clients' faces.

Those horrific events might have crushed a lesser woman. With two small girls to raise, Charlotte St. Sebastian wasted little time on self-pity. Once again she was forced to sell her heritage. The remaining jewels were discreetly disposed of over the years to provide her granddaughters with the education and lifestyle she insisted was their birthright. Private schools. Music tutors. Coming-out balls at the Waldorf. Smith College and a year at the Sorbonne for Sarah, Barnard for Gina.

Neither sister had a clue how desperate the financial situation had become, however, until Grandmama's heart attack. It was a mild one, quickly dismissed by the iron-spined duchess as a trifling bout of angina. The hospital charges weren't trifling, though. Nor was the stack of bills Sarah had found stuffed in Grandmama's desk when she sat down to pay what she'd thought were merely recurring monthly expenses. She'd nearly had a heart attack herself when she'd totaled up the amount.

Sarah had depleted her own savings account to pay that daunting stack of bills. Most of them, anyway. She still had to settle the charges for Grandmama's last echocardiogram. In the meantime, her single most important goal in life was to avoid stressing out the woman she loved with all her heart.

She let herself into their fifth-floor apartment, as shaken by Jerome's disclosure as by her earlier meeting with Devon Hunter. The comfortably padded Ecuadoran who served as maid, companion to Charlotte and friend to both Sarah and her sister for more than a decade was just preparing to leave.

"*Hola,* Sarah."

"*Hola,* Maria. How was your day?"

"Good. We walked, *la duquesa* and me, and shopped a little." She shouldered her hefty tote bag. "I go to catch my bus now. I'll see you tomorrow."

"Good night."

When the door closed behind her, a rich soprano voice only slightly dimmed by age called out, "Sarah? Is that you?"

"Yes, Grandmama."

She deposited her purse on the gilt-edged rococo sideboard gracing the entryway and made her way down a hall tiled in pale pink Carrara marble. The duchess hadn't been reduced to selling the furniture and artwork she'd acquired when she'd first arrived in New York, although Sarah now knew how desperately close she'd come to it.

"You're home early."

Charlotte sat in her favorite chair, the single aperitif she allowed herself despite the doctor's warning close at hand. The sight of her faded blue eyes and aristocratic nose brought a rush of emotion so strong Sarah had to swallow before she could a reply past the lump in her throat.

"Yes, I am."

She should have known Charlotte would pick up on the slightest nuance in her granddaughter's voice.

"You sound upset," she said with a small frown. "Did something happen at work?"

"Nothing more than the usual." Sarah forced a wry smile and went to pour herself a glass of white wine. "Alexis was on a tear about the ski-resort mock-up. I had to rework everything but the page count."

The duchess sniffed. "I don't know why you work for that woman."

"Mostly because she was the only one who would hire me."

"She didn't hire you. She hired your title."

Sarah winced, knowing it was true, and her grandmother instantly shifted gears.

"Lucky for Alexis the title came with an unerring eye for form, shape and spatial dimension," she huffed.

"Lucky for *me*," Sarah countered with a laugh. "Not everyone can parlay a degree in Renaissance-era art into a job at one of the country's leading fashion magazines."

"Or work her way from junior assistant to senior editor in just three years," Charlotte retorted. Her face softened into an expression that played on Sarah's heartstrings like a finely tuned Stradivarius. "Have I told you how proud I am of you?"

"Only about a thousand times, Grandmama."

They spent another half hour together before Charlotte decided she would rest a little before dinner. Sarah knew better than to offer to help her out of her chair, but she wanted to. God, she wanted to! When her grandmother's cane had thumped slowly down the hall to her bedroom, Sarah fixed a spinach salad and added a bit more liquid to the chicken Maria had begun baking in the oven. Then she washed her hands, detoured into the cavernous sitting room that served as a study and booted up her laptop.

She remembered the basics from the article *Beguile* had run on Devon Hunter. She wanted to dig deeper, uncover every minute detail she could about the man before she crossed swords with him again tomorrow evening.

Two

Seated at a linen-draped table by the window, Dev watched Sarah St. Sebastian approach the restaurant's entrance. Tall and slender, she moved with restrained grace. No swinging hips, no ground-eating strides, just a smooth symmetry of motion and dignity.

She wore her hair down tonight. He liked the way the mink-dark waves framed her face and brushed the shoulders of her suit jacket. The boxy jacket was a sort of pale purple. His sisters would probably call that color lilac or heliotrope or something equally girlie. The skirt was black and just swished her boot tops as she walked.

Despite growing up with four sisters, Dev's fashion sense could be summed up in a single word. A woman either looked good, or she didn't. This one looked good. *Very* good.

He wasn't the only one who thought so. When she entered the restaurant and the greeter escorted her to the table by the window, every head in the room turned. Males without female companions were openly admiring. Those with women at their tables were more discreet but no less appreciative. Many of the women, too, slanted those seemingly casual, careless glances that instantly catalogued every detail of hair, dress, jewelry and shoes.

How the hell did they do that? Dev could walk into the belly of a plane and tell in a single glance if the struts were buckling or the rivets starting to rust. As he'd discovered since that damned magazine article came out, however, his powers of observation paled beside those of the female of the species.

He'd treated the Ten Sexiest Singles list as a joke at first. He could hardly do otherwise, with his sisters, brothers-in-law and assorted nieces and nephews ragging him about it nonstop. And okay, being named one of the world's top ten hunks did kind of puff up his ego.

That was before women began stopping him on the street to let him know they were available. Before waitresses started hustling over to take his order and make the same pronouncement. Before the cocktail parties he was forced to attend as the price of doing business became a total embarrassment.

Dev had been able to shrug off most of it. He couldn't shrug off the wife of the French CEO he was trying to close a multibillion dollar deal with. The last time Dev was in Paris, Elise Girault had draped herself all over him. He knew then he had to put a stop to what had become more than just a nuisance.

He'd thought he'd found the perfect tool in Lady Eugenia Amalia Therése St. Sebastian. The blonde was gorgeous, vivacious and so photogenic that the vultures otherwise known as paparazzi wouldn't even glance at Dev if she was anywhere in the vicinity.

Thirty minutes in Gina St. Sebastian's company had deep-sixed that idea. Despite her pedigree, the woman was as bubbleheaded as she was sumptuous. Then she'd lifted the Byzantine medallion and the game plan had changed completely. For the better, Dev decided as he rose to greet the slender brunette being escorted to his table.

Chin high, shoulders back, Sarah St. Sebastian carried herself like the royalty she was. Or would have been, if her grandmother's small Eastern European country hadn't dispensed with royal titles about the same time Soviet tanks had rumbled across its border. The tanks had rumbled out again four decades later. By that time the borders of Eastern Europe had been redrawn several times and the duchy that had been home to the St. Sebastians for several centuries had completely disappeared.

Bad break for Charlotte St. Sebastian and her granddaughters. Lucky break for Dev. Lady Sarah didn't know it yet, but she was going to extract him from the mess she and her magazine had created.

"Good evening, Mr. Hunter."

The voice was cool, the green eyes cold.

"Good evening, Ms. St. Sebastian."

Dev stood patiently while the greeter seated her. A server materialized instantly.

"A cocktail or glass of wine before dinner, madam?"

"No, thank you. And no dinner." She waved aside the gilt-edged menu he offered and locked those forest-glade eyes on Dev. "I'll just be here a few minutes, then I'll leave Mr. Hunter to enjoy his meal."

The server departed, and Dev reclaimed his seat. "Are you sure you don't want dinner?"

"I'm sure." She placed loosely clasped hands on the table and launched an immediate offensive. "We're not here to exchange pleasantries, Mr. Hunter."

Dev sat back against his chair, his long legs outstretched beneath the starched tablecloth and his gaze steady on her face. Framed by those dark, glossy waves, her features fascinated him. The slight widow's peak, the high cheekbones, the aquiline nose—all refined and remote and in seeming contrast to those full, sensual lips. She might have modeled for some famous fifteenth- or sixteenth-century sculptor. Dev was damned if he knew which.

"No, we're not," he agreed, still intrigued by that face. "Have you talked to your sister?"

The clasped hands tightened. Only a fraction, but that small jerk was a dead giveaway.

"I haven't been able to reach her."

"Neither have I. So what do you propose we do now?"

"I propose you wait." She drew in a breath and forced a small smile. "Give me more time to track Gina down before you report your medallion missing or...or..."

"Or stolen?"

The smile evaporated. "Gina didn't steal that piece, Mr. Hunter. I admit it appears she took it for some reason, but I'm sure...I *know* she'll return it. Eventually."

Dev played with the tumbler containing his scotch, circling it almost a full turn before baiting the trap.

"The longer I wait to file a police report, Ms. St. Sebastian, the more my insurance company is going to question why. A delay reporting the loss could void the coverage."

"Give me another twenty-four hours, Mr. Hunter. Please."

She hated to beg. He heard it in her voice, saw it in the way her hands were knotted together now, the knuckles white.

"All right, Ms. St. Sebastian. Twenty-four hours. If your sister hasn't returned the medallion by then, however, I..."

"She will. I'm sure she will."

"And if she doesn't?"

She drew in another breath: longer, shakier. "I'll pay you the appraised value."

"How?"

Her chin came up. Her jaws went tight. "It will take some time," she admitted. "We'll have to work out a payment schedule."

Dev didn't like himself much at the moment. If he didn't have a multibillion-dollar deal hanging fire, he'd call this farce off right now. Setting aside the crystal tumbler, he leaned forward.

"Let's cut to the chase here, Ms. St. Sebastian. I had my people run an in-depth background check on your feather-headed sister. On you, too. I know you've bailed Gina out of one mess after another. I know you're currently providing your grandmother's sole support. I also know you barely make enough to cover her medical co-pays, let alone re-imburse me for a near-priceless artifact."

Every vestige of color had drained from her face, but pride sparked in those mesmerizing eyes. Before she could tell him where to go and how to get there, Dev sprang the trap.

"I have an alternate proposal, Ms. St. Sebastian."

Her brows snapped together. "What kind of a proposal?"

"I need a fiancée."

For the second time in as many days Dev saw her composure crumble. Her jaw dropping, she treated him to a disbelieving stare.

"Excuse me?"

"I need a fiancée," he repeated. "I was considering Gina for the position. I axed that idea after thirty minutes in her company. Becoming engaged to your sister," he drawled, "is not for the faint of heart."

He might have stunned her with his proposition. That didn't prevent her from leaping to the defense. Dev suspected it came as natural to her as breathing.

"My sister, Mr. Hunter, is warm and generous and open-hearted and…"

"Gone to ground." He drove the point home with the same swift lethality he brought to the negotiating table. "You, on the other hand, are available. And you owe me."

"*I* owe you?"

"You and that magazine you work for." Despite his best efforts to keep his irritation contained, it leaked into his voice. "Do you have any idea how many women have accosted me since that damned article came out? I can't even grab a meatball sub at my favorite deli without some female writing her number on a napkin and trying to stuff it into my pants pocket."

Her shock faded. Derision replaced it. She sat back in her chair with her lips pooched in false sympathy.

"Ooh. You poor, poor sex object."

"You may think it's funny," he growled. "I don't. Not with a multibillion-dollar deal hanging in the balance."

That wiped the smirk off her face. "Putting you on our Ten Sexiest Singles list has impacted your business? How?"

Enlightenment dawned in almost the next breath. The smirk returned. "Oh! Wait! I've got it. You have so many women throwing themselves at you that you can't concentrate."

"You're partially correct. But it's not a matter of not being able to concentrate. It's more that I don't want to jeopardize the deal by telling the wife of the man I'm negotiating with to keep her hands to herself."

"So instead of confronting the woman, you want to hide behind a fiancée."

The disdain was cool and well-bred, but it was there. Dev was feeling the sting when he caught a flutter of movement from the corner of one eye. A second later the flutter evolved into a tall, sleek redhead being shown to an empty table a little way from theirs. She caught Dev's glance, arched a penciled brow and came to a full stop beside their table.

"I know you." She tilted her head and put a finger to her chin. "Remind me. Where have we met?"

"We haven't," Dev replied, courteous outside, bracing inside.

"Are you sure? I never forget a face. Or," she added as her lips curved in a slow, feline smile, "a truly excellent butt."

The grimace that crossed Hunter's face gave Sarah a jolt

of fierce satisfaction. Let him squirm, she thought glee-fully. Let him writhe like a specimen under a microscope. He deserved the embarrassment.

Except…

He didn't. Not really. *Beguile* had put him under the mi-croscope. *Beguile* had also run a locker-room photo with the face angled away from the camera just enough to keep them from getting sued. And as much as Sarah hated to admit it, the man had shown a remarkable degree of re-straint by not reporting his missing artifact to the police immediately.

Still, she didn't want to come to his rescue. She *really* didn't. It was an innate and very grudging sense of fair play that compelled her to mimic her grandmother in one of Charlotte's more imperial moods.

"I beg your pardon," she said with icy hauteur. "I be-lieve my fiancé has already stated he doesn't know you. Now, if you don't mind, we would like to continue our conversation."

The woman's cheeks flushed almost the same color as her hair. "Yes, of course. Sorry for interrupting."

She hurried to her table, leaving Hunter staring after her while Sarah took an unhurried sip from her water goblet.

"That's it." He turned back to her, amusement slashing across his face. "That's exactly what I want from you."

Whoa! Sarah gripped the goblet's stem and tried to blunt the impact of the grin aimed in her direction. Devon Hunter all cold and intimidating she could handle. Devon Hunter with crinkly squint lines at the corners of those killer blue eyes and his mouth tipped into a rakish smile was some-thing else again.

The smile made him look so different. That, and the more casual attire he wore tonight. He was in a suit again, but he'd dispensed with a tie and his pale blue shirt was open at the neck. This late in the evening, a five-o'clock shadow darkened his cheeks and chin, giving him the sophisticated bad-boy look so many of *Beguile*'s male models tried for but could never quite pull off.

The research Sarah had done on the man put him in a different light, too. She'd had to dig hard for details. Hunter was notorious about protecting his privacy, which was why *Beguile* had been forced to go with a fluff piece instead of the in-depth interview Alexis had wanted. And no doubt why he resented the article so much, Sarah acknowledged with a twinge of guilt.

The few additional details she'd managed to dig up had contributed to an intriguing picture. She'd already known that Devon Hunter had enlisted in the Air Force right out of high school and trained as a loadmaster on big cargo jets. She hadn't known he'd completed a bachelor's *and* a master's during his eight years in uniform, despite spending most of those years flying into combat zones or disaster areas.

On one of those combat missions his aircraft had come under intense enemy fire. Hunter had jerry-rigged some kind of emergency fix to its damaged cargo ramp that had allowed them to take on hundreds of frantic Somalian refugees attempting to escape certain death. He'd left the Air Force a short time later and patented the modification he'd devised. From what Sarah could gather, it was now used on military and civilian aircraft worldwide.

That enterprise had earned Hunter his first million. The rest, as they say, was history. She hadn't found a precise estimate of the man's net worth, but it was obviously enough to allow him to collect hundred-thousand-pound museum pieces. Which brought her back to the problem at hand.

"Look, Mr. Hunter, this whole…"

"Dev," he interrupted, the grin still in place. "Now that we're engaged, we should dispense with the formalities. I know you have a half-dozen names. Do you go by Sarah or Elizabeth or Marie-Adele?"

"Sarah," she conceded, "but we are *not* engaged."

He tipped his chin toward the woman several tables away, her nose now buried in a menu. "Red there thinks we are."

"I simply didn't care for her attitude."

"Me, either." The amusement left his eyes. "That's why I offered you a choice. Let me spell out the basic terms so there's no misunderstanding. You agree to an engagement. Six months max. Less, if I close the deal currently on the table. In return, I destroy the surveillance tape and don't report the loss."

"But the medallion! You said it was worth a hundred thousand pounds or more."

"I'm willing to accept your assurances that Gina will return it. Eventually. In the meantime…" He lifted his tumbler in a mock salute. "To us, Sarah."

Feeling much like the proverbial mouse backed into a corner, she snatched at her last lifeline. "You promised me another twenty-four hours. The deal doesn't go into effect until then. Agreed?"

He hesitated, then lifted his shoulders in a shrug. "Agreed."

Surely Gina would return her calls before then and this whole, ridiculous situation would be resolved. Sarah clung to that hope as she pushed away from the table.

"Until tomorrow, Mr. Hunter."

"Dev," he corrected, rising, as well.

"No need for you to walk me out. Please stay and enjoy your dinner."

"Actually, I got hungry earlier and grabbed a Korean taco from a street stand. Funny," he commented as he tossed some bills on the table, "I've been in and out of Korea a dozen times. Don't remember ever having tacos there."

He took her elbow in a courteous gesture Grandmama would approve of. Very correct, very polite, not really possessive but edging too close to it for Sarah's comfort. Walking beside him only reinforced the impression she'd gained yesterday of his height and strength.

They passed the redhead's table on the way to the door. She glanced up, caught Sarah's dismissive stare and stuck her nose back in the menu.

"I'll hail you a cab," Hunter said as they exited the restaurant.

"It's only a few blocks."

"It's also getting dark. I know this is your town, but I'll feel better sending you home in a cab."

Sarah didn't argue further, mostly because dusk had started to descend and the air had taken on a distinct chill. Across the street, the lanterns in Central Park shed their golden glow. She turned in a half circle, her artist's eye delighting in the dots of gold punctuating the deep purple of the park.

Unfortunately, the turn brought the redhead into view again. The picture there wasn't as delightful. She was squinting at them through the restaurant's window, a phone jammed to her ear. Whoever she was talking to was obviously getting an earful.

Sarah guessed instantly she was spreading the word about Sexy Single Number Three and his fiancée. The realization gave her a sudden, queasy feeling. New York City lived and breathed celebrities. They were the stuff of life on *Good Morning America,* were courted by Tyra Banks and the women of *The View,* appeared regularly on *Late Show with David Letterman.* The tabloids, the glossies, even the so-called "literary" publications paid major bucks for inside scoops.

And Sarah had just handed them one. Thoroughly disgusted with herself for yielding to impulse, she smothered a curse that would have earned a sharp reprimand from Grandmama. Hunter followed her line of sight and spotted the woman staring at them through the restaurant window, the phone still jammed to her ear. He shared Sarah's pessimistic view of the matter but didn't bother to swallow his curse. It singed the night air.

"This is going turn up in another rag like *Beguile,* isn't it?"

Sarah stiffened. True, she'd privately cringed at some of the articles Alexis had insisted on putting in print. But that didn't mean she would stand by and let an outsider disparage her magazine.

"*Beguile* is hardly a rag. We're one of the leading fashion publications for women in the twenty to thirty-five age range, here and abroad."

"If you say so."

"I do," she ground out.

The misguided sympathy she'd felt for the man earlier had gone as dry and stale as yesterday's bagel. It went even staler when he turned to face her. Devon Hunter of the crinkly squint lines and heart-stuttering grin was gone. His intimidating alter ego was back.

"I guess if we're going to show up in some pulp press, we might as well give the story a little juice."

She saw the intent in his face and put up a warning palm. "Let's not do anything rash here, Mr. Hunter."

"Dev," he corrected, his eyes drilling into hers. "Say it, Sarah. Dev."

"All right! Dev. Are you satisfied?"

"Not quite."

His arm went around her waist. One swift tug brought them hip to hip. His hold was an iron band, but he gave her a second, maybe two, to protest.

Afterward Sarah could list in precise order the reasons she should have done exactly that. She didn't like the man. He was flat-out blackmailing her with Gina's rash act. He was too arrogant, and too damned sexy, for his own good.

But right then, right there, she looked up into those

dangerous blue eyes and gave in to the combustible mix of guilt, nagging worry and Devon Hunter's potent masculinity.

Three

Sarah had been kissed before. A decent number of times, as a matter of fact. She hadn't racked up as many admirers as Gina, certainly, but she'd dated steadily all through high school and college. She'd also teetered dangerously close to falling in love at least twice. Once with the sexy Italian she'd met at the famed Uffizi Gallery and spent a dizzying week exploring Florence with. Most recently with a charismatic young lawyer who had his eye set on a career in politics. That relationship had died a rather painful death when she discovered he was more in love with her background and empty title than he was with her.

Even with the Italian, however, she'd never indulged in embarrassingly public displays of affection. In addition to Grandmama's black-and-white views of correct behavior, Sarah's inbred reserve shied away from the kind of exuberant joie de vivre that characterized her sister. Yet here she was, locked in the arms of a near stranger on the sidewalk of one of New York's busiest avenues. Her oh-so-proper self shouted that she was providing a sideshow for everyone in and outside the restaurant. Her other self, the one she let off its leash only on rare occasions, leaped to life.

If *Beguile* ever ran a list of the World's Ten Best Kissers, she thought wildly, she would personally nominate Devon Hunter for the top slot. His mouth fit over hers as though it was made to. His lips demanded a response.

Sarah gave it. Angling her head, she planted both palms on his chest. The hard muscles under his shirt and suit coat provided a feast of tactile sensations. The fine bristles scraping her chin added more. She could taste the faint, smoky hint of scotch on his lips, feel the heat that rose in his skin.

There was nothing hidden in Hunter's kiss. No attempt to impress or connect or score a victory in the battle of the sexes. His mouth moved easily over hers. Confidently. Hungrily.

Her breath came hard and fast when he raised his head. So did his. Sarah took immense satisfaction in that—and the fact that he looked as surprised and disconcerted as she felt at the moment. When his expression switched to a frown, though, she half expected a cutting remark. What she got was a curt apology.

"I'm sorry." He dropped his hold on her waist and stepped back a pace. "That was uncalled for."

Sarah wasn't about to point out that she hadn't exactly resisted. While she struggled to right her rioting senses, she caught a glimpse of a very interested audience backlit inside the restaurant. Among them was the redhead, still watching avidly, only this time she had her phone aimed in their direction.

"Uncalled for or not," Sarah said with a small groan, "be prepared for the possibility that kiss might make its way into print. I suspect your friend's phone is camera equipped."

He shot a glance over his shoulder and blew out a disgusted breath. "I'm sure it is."

"What a mess," she murmured half under her breath. "My boss will *not* be happy."

Hunter picked up on the ramifications of the comment instantly. "Is this going to cause a problem for you at work? You and me, our engagement, getting scooped by some other rag, uh, magazine?"

"First, we're not engaged. Yet. Second, you don't need to worry about my work."

Mostly because he wouldn't be on scene when the storm hit. If *Beguile*'s executive editor learned from another source that Sarah had locked lips with Number Three on busy Central Park West, she'd make a force-five hurricane seem like a spring shower.

Then there was the duchess.

"I'm more concerned about my grandmother," Sarah admitted reluctantly. "If she should see or hear something before I get this mess straightened out..."

She gnawed on her lower lip, trying to find a way out of what was looking more and more like the kind of dark, tangly thing you find at the bottom of a pond. To her surprise, Hunter offered a solution to at least one of her problems.

"Tell you what," he said slowly. "Why don't I take you home tonight? You can introduce me to your grandmother. That way, whatever happens next won't come as such a bolt from the blue."

It was a measure of how desperate Sarah was feeling that she actually considered the idea.

"I don't think so," she said after a moment. "I don't want to complicate the situation any more at this point."

"All right. I'm staying at the Waldorf. Call me when you've had time to consider my proposal. If I don't hear from you within twenty-four hours, I'll assume your tacit agreement."

With that parting shot, he stepped to the curb and flagged down a cab for her. Sarah slid inside, collapsed against the seat and spent the short ride to the Dakota alternately feeling the aftereffects of that kiss, worrying about her sister and cursing the mess Gina had landed her in.

When she let herself in to the apartment, Maria was emptying the dishwasher just prior to leaving.

"*Hola,* Sarah."

"*Hola,* Maria. How did it go today?"

"Well. We walk in the park this afternoon."

She tucked the last plate in the cupboard and let the dishwasher close with a quiet whoosh. The marble counter got a final swipe.

"We didn't expect you home until late," the housekeeper commented as she reached for the coat she'd draped over a kitchen chair. "*La duquesa* ate an early dinner and retired to her room. She dozed when I checked a few minutes ago."

"Okay, Maria. Thanks."

"You're welcome, *chica.*" The Ecuadoran shrugged into her coat and hefted her suitcase-size purse. Halfway to the hall, she turned back. "I almost forgot. Gina called."

"When!"

"About a half hour ago. She said you texted her a couple times."

"A couple? Try ten or twenty."

"Ah, well." A fond smile creased the maid's plump cheeks. "That's Gina."

"Yes, it is," Sarah agreed grimly. "Did she mention where she was?"

"At the airport in Los Angeles. She said she just wanted to make sure everything was all right before she got on the plane."

"What plane? Where was she going?"

Maria's face screwed up in concentration. "Switzerland, I think she said. Or maybe…Swaziland?"

Knowing Gina, it could be either. Although, Sarah thought on a sudden choke of panic, Europe probably boasted better markets for twelfth-century Byzantine artifacts.

She said a hurried good-night to Maria and rummaged

frantically in her purse for her phone. She had to catch her sister before her plane took off.

When she got the phone out, the little green text icon indicated she had a text message. And she'd missed hearing the alert. Probably because she was too busy letting Devon Hunter kiss her all the way into next week.

The message was brief and typical Gina.

Met the cuddliest ski instructor.
Off to Switzerland. Later.

Hoping against hope it wasn't too late, Sarah hit speed dial. The call went immediately to voice mail. She tried texting and stood beside the massive marble counter, scowling at the screen, willing the little icon to pop back a response.

No luck. Gina had obviously powered down her phone. If she ran true to form, she would forget to power the damned thing back up for hours—maybe days—after she landed in Switzerland.

Sarah could almost hear a loud, obnoxious clock ticking inside her head as she went to check on her grandmother. Hunter had given her an additional twenty-four hours. Twenty-three now, and counting.

She knocked lightly on the door, then opened it as quietly as she could. The duchess sat propped against a bank of pillows. Her eyes were closed and an open book lay in her lap.

The anxiety gnawing at Sarah's insides receded for a moment, edged aside by the love that filled her like liquid warmth. She didn't see her grandmother's thin, creased cheeks or the liver spots sprinkled across the back of her hands. She saw the woman who'd opened her heart and her arms to two scared little girls. Charlotte St. Sebastian had nourished and educated them. She'd also shielded them from as much of the world's ugliness as she could. Now it was Sarah's turn to do the same.

She tried to ease the book out of the duchess's lax fingers without waking her. She didn't succeed. Charlotte's papery eyelids fluttered up. She blinked a couple of times to focus and smiled.

"How was your dinner?"

Sarah couldn't lie, but she could dodge a bit. "The restaurant was definitely up to your standards. We'll have to go there for your birthday."

"Never mind my birthday." She patted the side of the bed. "Sit down and tell me about this friend of Eugenia's. Do you think there's anything serious between them?"

Hunter was serious, all right. Just not in any way Charlotte would approve of.

"They're not more than casual acquaintances. In fact, Gina sent me a text earlier this evening. She's off to Switzerland with the cuddliest ski instructor. Her words, not mine."

"That girl," Charlotte huffed. "She'll be the death of me yet."

Not if Sarah could help it. The clock was pounding away inside her head, though. In desperation, she took Hunter's advice and decided to lay some tentative groundwork for whatever might come tomorrow.

"I actually know him better than Gina does, Grandmama."

"The ski instructor?"

"The man I met at the restaurant this evening. Devon Hunter." Despite everything, she had to smile. "You know him, too. He came in at Number Three on our Ten Sexiest Singles list."

"Oh, for heaven's sake, Sarah. You know I only peruse *Beguile* to gain an appreciation for your work. I don't pay any attention to the content."

"I guess it must have been Maria who dog-eared that particular section," she teased.

Charlotte tipped her aristocratic nose. The gesture was

instinctive and inbred and usually preceded a withering set-down. To Sarah's relief, the nose lowered a moment later and a smile tugged at her grandmother's lips.

"Is he as hot in real life as he is in print?"

"Hotter." She drew a deep mental breath. "Which is why I kissed him outside the restaurant."

"You kissed him? In public?" Charlotte *tch-tched,* but it was a halfhearted effort. Her face had come alive with interest. "That's so déclassé, dearest."

"Yes, I know. Even worse, there was a totally obnoxious woman inside the restaurant. She recognized Devon and made a rather rude comment. I suspect she may have snapped a picture or two. The kiss may well show up in some tabloid."

"I should hope not!"

Her lips thinning, the duchess contemplated that distasteful prospect for a moment before making a shrewd observation.

"Alexis will throw a world-class tantrum if something like this appears in any magazine but hers. You'd best forewarn her."

"I intend to." She glanced at the pillbox and crystal water decanter on the marble-topped nightstand. "Did you take your medicine?"

"Yes, I did."

"Are you sure? Sometimes you doze off and forget."

"I took it, Sarah. Don't fuss at me."

"It's my job to fuss." She leaned forward and kissed a soft, lily-of-the-valley-scented cheek. "Good night, Grandmama."

"Good night."

She got as far as the bedroom door. Close, so close, to making an escape. She had one hand on the latch when the duchess issued an imperial edict.

"Bring this Mr. Hunter by for drinks tomorrow evening, Sarah. I would like to meet him."

"I'm not certain what his plans are."

"Whatever they are," Charlotte said loftily, "I'm sure he can work in a brief visit."

Sarah went to sleep trying to decide which would be worse: entering into a fake engagement, informing Alexis that a tabloid might beat *Beguile* to a juicy story involving one of its own editors or continuing to feed her grandmother half-truths.

The first thing she did when she woke up the next morning was grab her cell phone. No text from Gina. No email. No voice message.

"You're a dead woman," she snarled at her absent sibling. "Dead!"

Throwing back the covers, she stomped to the bathroom. Like the rest of the rooms in the apartment, it was high ceilinged and trimmed with elaborate crown molding. Most of the fixtures had been updated over the years, but the tub was big and claw-footed and original. Sarah indulged in long, decadent soaks whenever she could. This morning she was too keyed up and in too much of a hurry for anything more than a quick shower.

Showered and blow-dried, she chose one of her grandmama's former favorites—a slate-gray Pierre Balmain minidress in a classic A-line. According to Charlotte, some women used to pair these thigh-skimming dresses with white plastic go-go boots. *She* never did, of course. Far too gauche. She'd gone with tasteful white stockings and Ferragamo pumps. Sarah opted for black tights, a pair of Giuseppi Zanottis she'd snatched up at a secondhand shoe store and multiple strands of fat faux pearls.

Thankfully, the duchess preferred a late, leisurely breakfast with Maria, so Sarah downed her usual bagel and black coffee and left for work with only a quick goodbye.

She got another reprieve at work. Alexis had called in to say she was hopping an early shuttle to Chicago for a short-notice meeting with the head of their publishing group. And to Sarah's infinite relief, a computer search of stories in print for the day didn't pop with either her name or a lurid blowup of her wrapped in Devon Hunter's arms.

That left the rest of the day to try to rationalize her unexpected reaction to his kiss and make a half-dozen futile attempts to reach Gina. All the while the clock marched steadily, inexorably toward her deadline.

Dev shot a glance at the bank of clocks lining one wall of the conference room. Four-fifteen. A little less than four hours to the go/no-go point.

He tuned out the tanned-and-toned executive at the head of the gleaming mahogany conference table. The man had been droning on for almost forty minutes now. His equally slick associates had nodded and ahemed and interjected several editorial asides about the fat military contract they were confident their company would win.

Dev knew better. They'd understated their start-up costs so blatantly the Pentagon procurement folks would laugh these guys out of the competition. Dev might have chalked this trip to NYC as a total waste of time if not for his meeting with Sarah St. Sebastian.

Based on the profile he'd had compiled on her, he'd expected someone cool, confident, levelheaded and fiercely loyal to both the woman who'd raised her and the sibling who gave her such grief. What he hadn't expected was her inbred elegance. Or the kick to his gut when she'd walked into the restaurant last night. Or the hours he'd spent afterward remembering her taste and her scent and the press of her body against his.

His visceral reaction to the woman could be a potential glitch in his plan. He needed a decoy. A temporary fiancée to blunt the effect of that ridiculous article. Someone to act as a buffer between him and the total strangers hitting on him everywhere he went—and the French CEO's wife who'd whispered such suggestive obscenities in his ear.

Sarah St. Sebastian was the perfect solution to those embarrassments. She'd proved as much last night when she'd cut Red off at the knees. Problem was the feel of her, the taste of her, had damned near done the same to Dev. The delectable Sarah could well prove more of a distraction than the rest of the bunch rolled up together.

So what the hell should he do now? Call her and tell her the deal he'd offered was no longer on the table? Write off the loss of the medallion? Track Gina down and recover the piece himself?

The artifact itself wasn't the issue, of course. Dev had lost more in the stock market in a single day than that bit of gold and enamel was worth. The only reason he'd pursued it this far was that he didn't like getting ripped off any more than the next guy. That, and the damned Ten Sexiest Singles article. He'd figured he could leverage the theft of the medallion into a temporary fiancée.

Which brought him full circle. What should he do about Sarah? His conscience had pinged at him last night. It was lobbing 50mm mortar shells now.

Dev had gained a rep in the multibillion-dollar world of aerospace manufacturing for being as tough as boot leather, but honest. He'd never lied to a competitor or grossly underestimated a bid like these jokers were doing now. Nor had he ever resorted to blackmail. Dev shifted uncomfortably, feeling as prickly about the one-sided deal he'd offered Sarah as by the patently false estimates Mr. Smooth kept flashing up on the screen.

To hell with it. He could take care of at least one of those itches right now.

"Excuse me, Jim."

Tanned-and-toned broke off in midspiel. He and his associates turned eager faces to Dev.

"We'll have to cut this short," he said without a trace of

apology. "I've got something hanging fire that I thought could wait. I need to take care of it now."

Jim and company concealed their disappointment behind shark-toothed smiles. Professional courtesy dictated that Devon offer a palliative.

"Why don't you email me the rest of your presentation? I'll study it on the flight home."

Tanned-and-toned picked up an in-house line and murmured an order to his AV folks. When he replaced the receiver, his smile sat just a few degrees off center.

"It's done, Dev."

"Thanks, Jimmy. I'll get back to you when I've had a chance to review your numbers in a little more depth."

Ole Jim's smile slipped another couple of degrees but he managed to hang on to its remnants as he came around the table to pump Devon's hand.

"I'll look forward to hearing from you. Soon, I hope."

"By the end of the week," Devon promised, although he knew Mr. Smooth wouldn't like what he had to say.

He decided to wait until he was in the limo and headed back to his hotel to contact Sarah. As the elevator whisked him down fifty stories, he tried to formulate exactly what he'd say to her.

His cell phone buzzed about twenty stories into the descent. Dev answered with his customary curt response, blissfully unaware a certain green-eyed brunette was just seconds away from knocking his world off its axis.

"Hunter."

"Mr. Hunter… Dev… It's Sarah St. Sebastian."

"Hello, Sarah. Have you heard from Gina?"

"Yes. Well, sort of."

Hell! So much for his nagging guilt over coercing this woman into a fake engagement. All Devon felt now was a searing disappointment that it might not take place. The feeling was so sharp and surprisingly painful he almost missed her next comment.

"Gina's on her way to Switzerland. Or she was when she texted me last night."

"What's in...?"

He broke off, knowing the answer before he asked the question. Bankers in Switzerland would commit hara-kiri before violating the confidentiality of deals brokered under their auspices. What better place to sell—and deposit the proceeds of—a near-priceless piece of antiquity?

"So where does that leave us?"

It came out stiffer than he'd intended. She responded in the same vein.

"I'm still trying to reach Gina. If I can't..."

The elevator reached the lobby. Dev stepped out, the phone to his ear and his adrenaline pumping the way it did when his engineers were close to some innovative new concept or major modification to the business of hauling cargo.

"If you can't?" he echoed.

"I don't see I have any choice but to agree to your preposterous offer."

She spelled it out. Slowly. Tightly. As if he'd forgotten the conditions he'd laid down last night.

"Six months as your fiancée. Less if you complete the negotiations you're working on. In return, you don't press charges against my sister. Correct?"

"Correct." Crushing his earlier doubts, he pounced. "So we have a deal?"

"On one condition."

A dozen different contingency clauses flashed through his mind. "And that is?" he said cautiously.

"You have to come for cocktails this evening. Seven o'clock. My grandmother wants to meet you."

Four

Dev frowned at his image in the elevator's ornate mirror and adjusted his tie. He was damned if he knew why he was so nervous about meeting Charlotte St. Sebastian.

He'd flown into combat zones more times than he could count, for God's sake. He'd also participated in relief missions to countries devastated by fires, tsunamis, earthquakes, horrific droughts and bloody civil wars. More than once his aircraft had come under enemy fire. And he still carried the scar from the hit he'd taken while racing through a barrage of bullets to get a sobbing, desperate mother and her wounded child aboard before murderous rebels overran the airport.

Those experiences had certainly shaped Dev's sense of self. Building an aerospace design-and-manufacturing empire from the ground up only solidified that self-confidence. He now rubbed elbows with top-level executives and power brokers around the world. Charlotte St. Sebastian wouldn't be the first royal he'd met, or even the highest ranking.

Yet the facts Dev had gathered about the St. Sebastian family painted one hell of an intimidating picture of its matriarch. The woman had once stood next in line to rule

48 A BUSINESS ENGAGEMENT

a duchy with a history that spanned some seven hundred years. She'd been forced to witness her husband's execution by firing squad. Most of her remaining family had disappeared forever in the notorious gulags. Charlotte herself had gone into hiding with her infant daughter and endured untold hardships before escaping to the West.

That would be heartbreak enough for anyone. Yet the duchess had also been slammed with the tragic death of her daughter and son-in-law, then had raised her two young granddaughters alone. Few, if any, of her friends and acquaintances were aware that she maintained only the facade of what appeared to be a luxurious lifestyle. Dev knew because he'd made it his business to learn everything he could about the St. Sebastians after beautiful, bubbly Lady Eugenia had lifted the Byzantine medallion.

He could have tracked Gina down. Hell, anyone with a modicum of computer smarts could track a GPS-equipped cell phone these days. Dev had considered doing just that until he'd realized her elder sister was better suited for his purposes. Plus, there was the bonus factor of where Sarah St. Sebastian worked. It had seemed only fair that he get a little revenge for the annoyance caused by that article.

Except, he thought as he exited the elevator, revenge had a way of coming back to bite you in the ass. What had seemed like a solid plan when he'd first devised it was now generating some serious doubts. Could he keep his hands off the elegant elder sister and stick to the strict terms of their agreement? Did he want to?

The doubts dogged him right up until he pressed the button for the doorbell. He heard a set of melodic chimes, and his soon-to-be fiancée opened the door to him.

"Hello, Mr.... Dev."

She was wearing chunky pearls, a thigh-skimming little dress and black tights tonight. The pearls and gray dress gave her a personal brand of sophistication, but the tights showcased her legs in a way that made Dev's throat go bone-dry. He managed to untangle his tongue long enough to return her greeting.

"Hello, Sarah."

"Please, come in."

She stood aside to give him access to a foyer longer than the belly of a C-17 and almost as cavernous. Marble tiles, ornate wall sconces, a gilt-edged side table and a crystal bowl filled with something orange blossomy. Dev absorbed the details along with the warning in Sarah's green eyes.

"I've told my grandmother that you and Gina are no more than casual acquaintances," she confided in a low voice.

"That's true enough."

"Yes, well…" She drew in a breath and squared shoulders molded by gray silk. "Let's get this over with."

She led the way down the hall. Dev followed and decided the rear view was as great as the front. The dress hem swayed just enough to tease and tantalize. The tights clung faithfully to the curve of her calves.

He was still appreciating the view when she showed him into a high-ceilinged room furnished with a mix of antiques and a few pieces of modern technology. The floor here was parquet; the wood was beautifully inlaid, but cried for the cushioning of a soft, handwoven carpet to blunt some of its echo. Windows curtained in pale blue velvet took up most of two walls and gave what Dev guessed was one hell of a view of Central Park. Flames danced in the massive fireplace fronted in black marble that dominated a third wall.

A sofa was angled to catch the glow from the fire. Two high-backed armchairs faced the sofa across a monster coffee table inset with more marble. The woman on one of those chairs sat ramrod straight, with both palms resting on the handle of an ebony cane. Her gray hair was swept up into a curly crown and anchored by ivory combs. Lace wrapped her throat like a muffler and was anchored by a cameo brooch. Her hawk's eyes skewered Dev as he crossed the room.

Sarah summoned a bright smile and performed the introductions. "Grandmama, this is Devon Hunter."

"How do you do, Mr. Hunter?"

The duchess held out a veined hand. Dev suspected that courtiers had once dropped to a knee and kissed it reverently. He settled for taking it gently in his.

"It's a pleasure to meet you, ma'am. Gina told me she'd inherited her stunning looks from her grandmother. She obviously had that right."

"Indeed?" Her chin lifted. Her nose angled up a few degrees. "You know Eugenia well, then?"

"She coordinated a party for me. We spoke on a number of occasions."

"Do sit down, Mr. Hunter." She waved him to the chair across from hers. "Sarah, dearest, please pour Mr. Hunter a drink."

"Certainly. What would you like, Dev?"

"Whatever you and your grandmother are having is fine."

"I'm having white wine." Her smile tipped into one of genuine affection as she moved to a side table containing an opened bottle of wine nested in a crystal ice bucket and an array of decanters. "Grandmama, however, is ignoring her doctor's orders and sipping an abominable brew concocted by our ancestors back in the sixteenth century."

"*Žuta Osa* is hardly abominable, Sarah," the duchess countered. She lifted a tiny liqueur glass and swirled its amber-colored contents before treating her guest to a bland look. "It simply requires a strong constitution."

Dev recognized a challenge when one smacked him in the face. "I'll give it a try."

"Are you sure?" Sarah shot him a warning glance from behind the drinks table. "The name translates roughly to yellow wasp. That might give you an idea of what it tastes like."

"Really, Sarah! You must allow Mr. Hunter to form his own opinion of what was once our national drink."

Dev was already regretting his choice but concealed it behind a polite request. "Please call me Dev, ma'am."

He didn't presume to address the duchess by name or by rank. Mostly because he wasn't sure which came first. European titles were a mystery wrapped up in an enigma to most Americans. Defunct Eastern European titles were even harder to decipher. Dev had read somewhere that the form of address depended on whether the rank was inherited or bestowed, but that didn't help him a whole lot in this instance.

The duchess solved his dilemma when she responded to his request with a gracious nod. "Very well. And you may call me Charlotte."

Sarah paused with the stopper to one of the decanters in hand. Her look of surprise told Dev he'd just been granted a major concession. She recovered a moment later and filled one of the thimble-size liqueur glasses. Passing it to Dev, she refilled her wineglass and took a seat beside her grandmother.

As he lifted the glass in salute to his hostess, he told himself a half ounce of yellow wasp couldn't do much damage. One sip showed just how wrong he was. The fiery, plum-based liquid exploded in his mouth and damned near burned a hole in his esophagus.

"Holy sh…!"

He caught himself in time. Eyes watering, he held the glass at arm's length and gave the liqueur the respect it deserved. When he could breathe again, he met the duchess's amused eyes.

"This puts the stuff we used to brew in our helmets in Iraq to shame."

"You were in Iraq?" With an impatient shake of her

head, Charlotte answered her own question. "Yes, of course you were. Afghanistan, too, if I remember correctly from the article in *Beguile*."

Okay, now he was embarrassed. The idea of this gray-haired matriarch reading all that nonsense—and perusing the picture of his butt crack!—went down even rougher than the liqueur.

To cover his embarrassment, Dev took another sip. The second was a little easier than the first but still left scorch marks all the way to his gullet.

"So tell me," Charlotte was saying politely, "how long will you be in New York?"

"That depends," he got out.

"Indeed?"

The duchess did the nose-up thing again. She was good at it, Dev thought as he waited for the fire in his stomach to subside.

"On what, if I may be so bold to ask?"

"On whether you and your granddaughter will have dinner with me this evening. Or tomorrow evening."

His glance shifted to Sarah. The memory of how she'd fit against him, how her mouth had opened under his, hit with almost the same sucker punch as the *Žuta Osa*.

"Or any evening," he added, holding her gaze.

Sarah gripped her wineglass. She didn't have any trouble reading the message in his eyes. It was a personal challenge. A not-so-private caress. Her grandmother would have to be blind to miss either.

Okay. All right. She'd hoped this meeting would blunt the surprise of a sudden engagement. Dev had done his part. The ball was now in her court.

"I can't speak for Grandmama, but I'm free tomorrow evening. Or any evening," she added with what felt like a silly, simpering smile.

She thought she'd overplayed her hand. Was sure of it when the duchess speared her with a sharp glance.

The question in her grandmother's eyes ballooned Sarah's guilt and worry to epic proportions. She couldn't do this. She couldn't deceive the woman who'd sold every precious family heirloom she owned to provide for her granddaughters. A confession trembled on her lips. The duchess forestalled it by turning back Devon Hunter.

"I'm afraid I have another engagement tomorrow evening."

Both women knew that to be a blatant lie. Too caught up in her own web of deceit to challenge her grandmother, Sarah tried not to squirm as the duchess slipped into the role of royal matchmaker.

"But I insist you take my granddaughter to dinner tomorrow. Or any evening," she added drily. "Right now, however, I'd like to know a little more about you."

Sarah braced herself. The duchess didn't attack with the same snarling belligerence as Alexis, but she was every bit as skilled and tenacious when it came to extracting information. Dev didn't stand a chance.

She had to admit he took the interrogation with good grace. Still, her nerves were stretched taunt when she went to bed some hours later. At least she'd mitigated the fallout from one potentially disastrous situation. If—*when*—she and Devon broke the news of their engagement, it wouldn't come as a complete shock to Grandmama.

She woke up the next morning knowing she had to defuse another potentially explosive situation. A quick scan of her phone showed no return call or text from Gina. An equally quick scan of electronic, TV and print media showed the story hadn't broken yet about Sarah and Number Three. It would, though. She sensed it with every instinct she'd developed after three years in the dog-eat-dog publishing business.

Alexis. She had to tell Alexis some version of her involvement with Devon Hunter. She tried out different slants as she hung from a handrail on the subway. Several more in the elevator that zoomed her up to *Beguile*'s offices. Every possible construction but one crumbled when Alexis summoned her into her corner office. Pacing like a caged tiger, the executive editor unleashed her claws.

"Jesus, Sarah!" Anger lowered Alexis's smoker's rasp to a frog-like croak. "You want to tell me why I have to hear secondhand that one of my editors swapped saliva with Sexy Single Number Three? On the street. In full view of every cabbie with a camera phone and an itch to sell a sensational story."

"Come on, Alexis. How many New York cabbies read *Beguile* enough to recognize Number Three?"

"At least one, apparently."

She flung the sheet of paper she was holding onto the slab of Lucite that was her desk. Sarah's heart tripped as she skimmed the contents. It was a printed email, and below the printed message was a grainy color photo of a couple locked in each other's arms. Sarah barely had time for a mental apology to Red for thinking she'd be the one to peddle the story before Alexis pounced.

"This joker wants five thousand for the picture."

"You're kidding!"

"See this face?" The executive editor stabbed a finger at her nose. "Does it look like I'm kidding?"

"This…this isn't what you think, Alexis."

"So maybe you'll tell me what the hell it is, Lady Sarah."

It might have been the biting sarcasm. Or the deliberate reference to her title. Or the worry about Gina or the guilt over lying to her grandmother or the pressure Devon Hunter had laid on her. Whatever caused Sarah's sudden meltdown, the sudden burst of tears shocked her as much as it did Alexis.

"Oh, Christ!" Her boss flapped her hands like a PMS-ing

hen. "I'm sorry. I didn't mean to come at you so hard. Well, maybe I did. But you don't have to cry about it."

"Yes," Sarah sobbed, "I do!"

The truth was she couldn't have stopped if she wanted to. All the stress, all the strain, seemed to boil out of her. Not just the problems that had piled up in the past few days. The months of worrying about Grandmama's health. The years of standing between Gina and the rest of the world. Everything just seemed to come to a head. Dropping into a chair, she crossed her arms on the half acre of unblemished Lucite and buried her face.

"Hey! It's okay." Alexis hovered over her, patting her shoulder, sounding more desperate and bullfroggish by the moment. "I'll sit on this email. Do what I can to kill the story before it leaks."

Sarah raised her head. She'd struck a deal. She'd stand by it. "You don't have to kill it. Hunter... He and I..."

"You and Hunter...?"

She dropped her head back onto her arms and gave a muffled groan. "We're engaged."

"What! When? Where? How?"

Reverting to her natural self, Alexis was relentless. Within moments she'd wormed out every succulent detail. Hunter's shocking accusation. The video with its incontrovertible proof. The outrageous proposal. The call from Gina stating that she was on her way to Switzerland.

"Your sister is a selfish little bitch," Alexis pronounced in disgust. "When are you going to stop protecting her?"

"Never!" Blinking away her tears, Sarah fired back with both barrels. "Gina's all I have. Gina and Grandmama. I'll do whatever's necessary to protect them."

"That's all well and good, but your sister..."

"*Is* my sister."

"Okay, okay." Alexis held up both palms. "She's your sister. And Devon Hunter's your fiancé for the next six months. Unless..."

Her face took on a calculating expression. One Sarah knew all too well. She almost didn't want to ask, but the faint hope that her boss might see a way out of the mess prompted a tentative query.

"Unless what?"

"What if you keep a journal for the next few weeks? Better yet, a photo journal?"

Deep in thought, Alexis tapped a bloodred nail against her lips. Sarah could almost see the layout taking shape in her boss's fertile mind.

"You and Hunter. The whirlwind romance. The surprise proposal. The romantic dinners for two. The long walks in Central Park. Our readers would eat it up."

"Forget it, Alexis. I'm not churning out more juicy gossip for our readers."

"Why not?"

The counter came as swift and as deadly as an adder. In full pursuit of a feature now, Alexis dropped into the chair next to Sarah and pressed her point.

"You and I both know celebrity gossip sells. And this batch comes with great bonus elements. Hunter's not only rich, but handsome as hell. You're a smart, savvy career woman with a connection to royalty."

"A connection to a royal house that doesn't exist anymore!"

"So? We resurrect it. Embellish it. Maybe send a photographer over to shoot some local color from your grandmother's homeland. Didn't you say you still had some cousins there?"

"Three or four times removed, maybe, but Grandmama hasn't heard from anyone there in decades."

"No problem. We'll make it work."

She saw the doubt on Sarah's face and pressed her point with ruthless determination.

"If what you give me is as full of glam and romance as I think it could be, it'll send our circulation through the roof. And that, my sweet, will provide you with enough of a bonus to reimburse Hunter for his lost artifact. *And* pay off the last of your grandmother's medical bills. *And* put a little extra in your bank account for a rainy day or two."

The dazzling prospect hung before Sarah's eyes for a brief, shining moment. She could extricate Gina from her latest mess. Become debt-free for the first time in longer than she could remember. Splurge on some totally unnecessary luxury for the duchess. Buy a new suit instead of retrofitting old classics.

She came within a breath of promising Alexis all the photos and R-rated copy she could print. Then her irritating sense of fair play raised its head.

"I can't do it," she said after a bitter internal struggle. "Hunter promised he wouldn't file charges against Gina if I play the role of adoring fiancée. I'll try to get him to agree to a photo shoot focusing on our—" she stopped, took a breath, continued "—on our engagement. I'm pretty sure he'll agree to that."

Primarily because it would serve his purpose. Once the word hit the street that he was taken, all those women shoving their phone numbers at him would just have to live with their disappointment. So would Alexis.

"That's as far as I'll go," Sarah said firmly.

Her boss frowned and was priming her guns for another salvo when her intercom buzzed. Scowling, she stabbed at the instrument on her desk.

"Didn't I tell you to hold all calls?"

"Yes, but…"

"What part of 'hold' don't you understand?"

"It's…"

"It's what, dammit?"

"Number Three," came the whispered reply. "He's here."

Five

If Dev hadn't just run past a gauntlet of snickering females, he might have been amused by the almost identical
expressions of surprise on the faces of his fiancée and her
boss. But he had, so he wasn't.

Alexis Danvers didn't help matters by looking him up
and down with the same scrutiny an auctioneer might give
a prize bull. As thin as baling wire, she sized him up with
narrowed, calculating eyes before thrusting out a hand
tipped with scarlet talons.

"Mr. Hunter. Good to meet you. Sarah says you and she
are engaged."

"Wish I could say the same, Ms. Danvers. And yes,
we are."

He shifted his gaze to Sarah, frowning when he noted
her reddened eyes and tearstained cheeks. He didn't have
to search far for the reason behind them. The grainy color
photo on Danvers's desk said it all.

Hell! Sarah had hinted the crap would hit the fan if some
magazine other than hers scooped the story. Looked as if
it had just hit. He turned back to the senior editor and vec-
tored the woman's anger in his direction.

"I'm guessing you might be a little piqued that Sarah didn't clue you in to our relationship before it became public knowledge."

Danvers dipped her chin in a curt nod. "You guessed right."

"I'm also guessing you understand why I wasn't real anxious for another avalanche of obnoxious publicity."

"If you're referring to the Ten Sexiest Singles article…"

"I am."

"Since you declined to let us interview you for that article, Mr. Hunter, everything we printed was in the public domain. Your military service. That cargo thingamajig you patented. Your corporation's profits last quarter. Your marital status. All we did was collate the facts, glam them up a little, toss in a few pictures and offer you to an admiring audience."

"Any more admiration from that audience and I'll have to hire a bodyguard."

"Or a fiancée?"

She slipped that in with the precision of a surgeon. Dev had to admire her skill even as he acknowledged the hit.

"Or a fiancée," he agreed. "Luckily I found the perfect one right here at *Beguile*."

Which reminded him of why he'd made a second trek to the magazine's offices.

"Something's come up," he told Sarah. "I was going to explain it to you privately, but…"

"You heard from Gina?"

Her breathless relief had Dev swearing silently. Little Miss Gina deserved a swift kick in the behind for putting her sister through all this worry. And he might just be the one to deliver it.

"No, I haven't."

The relief evaporated. Sarah's shoulders slumped. Only for a moment, though. The St. Sebastian steel reasserted itself almost immediately. Good thing, as she'd need every ounce of it for the sucker punch Dev was about to deliver.

"But I did hear from the CEO I've been negotiating with for the past few months. He's ready to hammer out the final details and asked me to fly over to Paris."

She sensed what was coming. He saw it in the widening of her green eyes, the instinctive shake of her head. Dev ignored both and pressed ahead.

"I told him I would. I also told him I might bring my fiancée. I explained we just got engaged, and that I'm thinking of taking some extra time so we can celebrate the occasion in his beautiful city."

"Excuse me!" Danvers butted in, her expression frigid. "Sarah has an important job here at *Beguile,* with deadlines to meet. She can't just flit off to Paris on your whim."

"I appreciate that. It would only be for a few days. Maybe a week."

Dev turned back to Sarah, holding her gaze, holding her to their bargain at the same time.

"We've been working this deal for months. I need to wrap it up. Monsieur Girault said his wife would be delighted to entertain you while we're tied up in negotiations."

He slipped in that veiled reminder of one of his touchiest problems deliberately. He'd been up front with her. He wanted her to provide cover from Elise Girault. In exchange, he'd let her light-fingered sister off the hook.

Sarah got the message. Her chin inched up. Her shoulders squared. The knowledge she would stick to her side of the bargain gave him a fiercer sense of satisfaction than he had time to analyze right now.

"When are you thinking of going?" she asked.

"My executive assistant has booked us seats on a seven-ten flight out of JFK."

"Tonight?"

"Tonight. You have a current passport, don't you?"

"Yes, but I can't just jet off and leave Grandmama!"

"Not a problem. I also had my assistant check with the top home health-care agencies in the city. A licensed, bonded RN can report for duty this afternoon and stay with your grandmother until you get back."

"Dear God, no!" A shudder shook her. "Grandmama would absolutely hate that invasion of her privacy. I'll ask our housekeeper, Maria, to stay with her."

"You sure?"

"I'm sure."

"Since I'm springing this trip on you with such short notice, please tell your housekeeper I'll recompense her for her time."

"That's not necessary," she said stiffly.

"Of course it is."

She started to protest, but Dev suggested a daily payment for Maria's services that made Sarah blink and her boss hastily intervene.

"The man's right, kiddo. This is his gig. Let him cover the associated costs."

She left unsaid the fact that Dev could well afford the generous compensation. It was right there, though, like the proverbial elephant in the room, and convinced Sarah to reluctantly agree.

"We're good to go, then."

"I…I suppose." She chewed on her lower lip for a moment. "I need to finish the Sizzling Summer Sea-escapes layout, Alexis."

"And the ad for that new lip gloss," her boss put in urgently. "I want it in the June edition."

"I'll take my laptop. I can do both layouts on the plane." She pushed out of her chair and faced Dev. "You understand that my accompanying you on this little jaunt is contingent on Maria's availability."

"I understand. Assuming she's available, can you be ready by three o'clock?"

"Isn't that a little early for a seven-ten flight?"

"It is, but we need to make a stop on the way out to JFK. Or would you rather go to Cartier now?"

"Cartier? Why do we…? Oh." She gave a low groan. "An engagement ring, right?"

"Right."

She shook her head in dismay. "This just keeps getting better and better."

Her boss took an entirely different view. With a hoarse whoop, she reached for the phone on her desk.

"Perfect! We'll send a camera crew to Cartier with you." She paused with the phone halfway to her ear and raked her subordinate with a critical glance. "Swing by makeup on your way out, Sarah. Have them ramp up your color. Wouldn't hurt to hit wardrobe, too. That's one of your grandmother's Dior suits, right? It's great, but it needs something. A belt, maybe. Or…"

Sarah cut in, alarm coloring her voice. "Hold on a minute, Alexis."

"What's to hold? This is exactly what we were talking about before Hunter arrived."

Sarah shot Dev a swift, guilty glance. It didn't take a genius for him to fill in the blanks. Obviously, her boss had been pressing to exploit the supposed whirlwind romance between one of her own and Number Three.

As much as it grated, Dev had to admit a splashy announcement of his engagement to Sarah St. Sebastian fell in with his own plans. If nothing else, it would get the word out that he was off the market and, hopefully, keep Madame Girault's claws sheathed.

"I'll consent to a few pictures, if that's what Sarah wants."

"A few pictures," she agreed with obvious reluctance, leveling a pointed look at her boss. "Just this *one* time."

"Come on, Sarah. How much more romantic can you get than April in Paris? The city of light and love. You and Hunter here strolling hand in hand along the Quai de Conti…"

"No, Alexis."

"Just think about it."

"No, Alexis."

There was something in the brief exchange Dev couldn't quite get a handle on. The communication between the two women was too emphatic, too terse. He didn't have time to decipher it now, however.

"Your people get this one shoot," he told Danvers, putting an end to the discussion. "They can do it at Cartier." He checked his watch. "Why don't you call your housekeeper now, Sarah? Make sure she's available. If she is, we'll put a ring on your finger and get you home to pack."

Sarah battled a headache as the limo cut through the Fifth Avenue traffic. Devon sat beside her on the cloud-soft leather, relaxed and seemingly unperturbed about throwing her life into total chaos. Seething, she threw a resentful glance at his profile.

Was it only two days ago he'd stormed into her life? Three? She felt as though she'd been broadsided by a semi. Okay, so maybe she couldn't lay all the blame for the situation she now found herself in on Dev. Gina had certainly contributed her share. Still…

When the limo pulled up at the front entrance to Cartier's iconic flagship store, the dull throb in her temples took on a sharper edge. With its red awnings and four stories of ultra high-end merchandise, the store was a New York City landmark.

Sarah hadn't discovered until after her grandmother's heart attack that Charlotte had sold a good portion of her jewels to Cartier over the years. According to a recent invoice, the last piece she'd parted with was still on display in their Estate Jewelry room.

Dev had called ahead, so they were greeted at the door

by the manager himself. "Good afternoon, Mr. Hunter. I'm Charles Tipton."

Gray-haired and impeccably attired, he shook Dev's hand before bowing over Sarah's with Old World courtesy.

"It's a pleasure to meet you, Ms. St. Sebastian. I've had the honor of doing business with your grandmother several times in the past."

She smiled her gratitude for his discretion. "Doing business with" stung so much less than "helping her dispose of her heritage."

"May I congratulate you on your engagement?"

She managed not to wince, but couldn't help thinking this lie was fast taking on a life of its own.

"Thank you."

"I'm thrilled, of course, that you came to Cartier to shop for your ring. I've gathered a selection of our finest settings and stones. I'm sure we'll find something exactly to your..."

He broke off as a cab screeched over to the curb and the crew from *Beguile* jumped out. Zach Zimmerman—nicknamed ZZ, of course—hefted his camera bags while his assistant wrestled with lights and reflectors.

"Hey, Sarah!" Dark eyed and completely irreverent about everything except his work, ZZ stomped toward them in his high-top sneakers. "You really engaged to Number Three or has Alexis been hitting the sauce again?"

She hid another wince. "I'm really engaged. ZZ, this is my fiancé, Devon..."

"Hunter. Yeah, I recognize the, uh, face."

He smirked but thankfully refrained from referring to any other part of Dev's anatomy.

"If you'll all please come with me."

Mr. Tipton escorted them through the first-floor show-room with its crystal chandeliers and alcoves framed with white marble arches. Faint strains of classical music floated on the air. The seductive scent of gardenia wafted from strategically positioned bowls of potpourri.

A short elevator ride took them to a private consultation room. Chairs padded in gold velvet were grouped on either side of a gateleg, gilt-trimmed escritoire. Several cases sparkling with diamond engagement sets sat on the desk's burled wood surface.

The manager gestured them to the chairs facing the desk but before taking his own he detoured to a sideboard holding a silver bucket and several Baccarat flutes.

"May I offer you some champagne? To toast your engagement, perhaps?"

Sarah glanced at Dev, saw he'd left the choice up to her, and surrendered to the inevitable.

"Thank you. That would be delightful."

The cork had already been popped. Tipton filled flutes and passed them to Sarah and Dev. She took the delicate crystal, feeling like the biggest fraud on earth. Feeling as well the stupidest urge to indulge in another bout of loud, sloppy tears.

Like many of *Beguile*'s readers, Sarah occasionally got caught up in the whole idea of romance. You could hardly sweat over layouts depicting the perfect engagement or wedding or honeymoon without constructing a few private fantasies. But this was about as far from those fantasies as she could get. A phony engagement. A pretend fiancé. A ring she would return as soon as she fulfilled the terms of her contract.

Then she looked up from the pale gold liquid bubbling in her flute and met Dev's steady gaze. His eyes had gone deep blue, almost cobalt, and something in their depths made her breath snag. When he lifted his flute and tipped it to hers, the fantasies begin to take on vague form and shape.

"To my…" he began.

"Wait!" ZZ pawed through his camera bag. "I need to catch this."

The moment splintered. Like a skater on too-thin ice,

Sarah felt the cracks spidering out beneath her feet. Panic replaced the odd sensation of a moment ago. She had to fight the urge to slam down the flute and get off the ice before she sank below the surface.

She conquered the impulse, but couldn't summon more than a strained smile once ZZ framed the shot.

"Okay," the photographer said from behind a foot-long lens, "go for it!"

Dev's gesture with his flute was the same. So was the caress in his voice. But whatever Sarah had glimpsed in his blue eyes a moment ago was gone.

"To us," he said as crystal clinked delicately against crystal.

"To us," she echoed.

She took one sip, just one, and nixed ZZ's request to repeat the toast so he could shoot it from another angle. She couldn't ignore him or his assistant, however, while she tried on a selection of rings. Between them, they made the process of choosing a diamond feel like torture.

According to Tipton, Dev had requested a sampling of rings as refined and elegant as his fiancée. Unfortunately, none of the glittering solitaires he lifted from the cases appealed to Sarah. With an understanding nod, he sent for cases filled with more elaborate settings.

Once again Sarah could almost hear a clock ticking inside her head. She needed to make a decision, zip home, break the startling news of her engagement to Grandmama, get packed and catch that seven-ten flight. Yet none of the rings showcased on black velvet triggered more than a tepid response.

Like it mattered. Just get this over with, she told herself grimly.

She picked up a square cut surrounded by glittering baguettes. Abruptly, she returned it to the black velvet pad.

"I think I would prefer something unique." She looked Tipton square in the eye. "Something from your estate sales, perhaps. An emerald, for my birth month. Mounted in gold."

Her birthday was in November, and the stone for that month was topaz. She hoped Hunter hadn't assimilated that bit of trivia. The jeweler had, of course, but he once again proved himself the soul of discretion.

"I believe we might have just the ring for you."

He lifted a house phone and issued a brief instruction. Moments later, an assistant appeared and deposited an intricately wrought ring on the display pad.

Thin ropes of gold were interwoven to form a wide band. An opaque Russian emerald nested in the center of the band. The milky green stone was the size and shape of a small gumball. When Sarah turned the ring over, she spotted a rose carved into the stone's flat bottom.

Someone with no knowledge of antique jewelry might scrunch their noses at the overly fussy setting and occluded gemstone. All Sarah knew was that she had to wear Grandmama's last and most precious jewel, if only for a week or so. Her heart aching, she turned to Dev.

"This is the one."

He tried to look pleased with her choice but didn't quite get there. The price the manager quoted only increased his doubts. Even fifteen-karat Russian emeralds didn't come anywhere close to the market value of a flawless three- or four-karat diamond.

"Are you sure this is the ring you want?"

"Yes."

Shrugging, he extracted an American Express card from his wallet. When Tipton disappeared to process the card, he picked up the ring and started to slip it on Sarah's finger.

ZZ stopped him cold. "Hold it!"

Dev's blue eyes went glacial. "Let us know when you're ready."

"Yeah, yeah, just hang on a sec."

ZZ thrust out a light meter, scowled at the reading and

barked orders to his assistant. After a good five minutes spent adjusting reflectors and falloff lights, they were finally ready.

"Go," the photographer ordered.

Dev slipped the ring on Sarah's finger. It slid over her knuckle easily, and the band came to rest at the base of her finger as though it had been sized especially for her.

"Good. Good." ZZ clicked a dozen fast shots. "Look up at him, Sarah. Give him some eye sex."

Heat rushed into her cheeks but she lifted her gaze. Dev wore a cynical expression for a second or two before exchanging it for one more lover-like.

Lights heated the room. Reflectors flashed. The camera shutter snapped and spit.

"Good. Good. Now let's have the big smooch. Make it hot, you two."

Tight lines appeared at the corners of Dev's mouth. For a moment he looked as though he intended to tell ZZ to take his zoom lens and shove it. Then he rose to his feet with lazy grace and held out a hand to Sarah.

"We'll have to try this without an audience sometime," he murmured as she joined him. "For now, though…"

She was better prepared this time. She didn't stiffen when he slid an arm around her waist. Didn't object when he curled his other hand under her chin and tipped her face to his. Yet the feel of his mouth, the taste and the scent of him, sent tiny shock waves rippling through her entire body.

A lyric from an old song darted into her mind. Something about getting lost in his kiss. That was exactly how she felt as his mouth moved over hers.

"Good. Good."

More rapid-fire clicks, more flashes. Finally ZZ was done. He squinted at the digital screen and ran through the entire sequence of images before he gave a thumbs-up.

"Got some great shots here. I'll edit 'em and email you

the best, Sarah. Just be sure to credit me if you use 'em on your bridal website."

Right. Like that was going to happen. Still trying to recover from her second session in Devon Hunter's arms, Sarah merely nodded.

While ZZ and his assistant packed up, Dev checked his watch. "Do you want to grab lunch before I take you home to pack?"

Sarah thought for a moment. Her number-one priority right now was finding some way to break the news to the duchess that her eldest granddaughter had become engaged to a man she'd met only a few days ago. She needed a plausible explanation. One that wouldn't trigger Charlotte's instant suspicion. Or worse, so much worse, make her heart stutter.

Sarah's glance dropped to the emerald. The stone's cloudy beauty gave her the bravado to respond to Dev's question with a completely false sense of confidence.

"Let's have lunch with Grandmama and Maria. We'll make it a small celebration in honor of the occasion, then I'll pack."

Six

Dev had employed a cautious, scope-out-the-territory approach for his first encounter with the duchess. For the second, he decided on a preemptive strike. As soon as he and Sarah were in the limo and headed uptown, he initiated his plan of attack.

"Do you need to call your grandmother and let her know we're coming?"

"Yes, I should." She slipped her phone out of her purse. "And I'll ask Maria to put together a quick lunch."

"No need. I'll take care of that. Does the duchess like caviar?"

"Yes," Sarah replied, a question in her eyes as he palmed his own phone, "but only Caspian Sea osetra. She thinks beluga is too salty and sevruga too fishy."

"What about Maria? Does she have a favorite delicacy?"

She had to think for a moment. "Well, on All Saints Day she always makes *fiambre*."

"What's that?"

"A chilled salad with fifty or so ingredients. Why?" she asked as he hit a speed-dial key. "What are you…?"

He held up a hand, signaling her to wait, and issued a

quick order. "I need a champagne brunch for four, delivered to Ms. St. Sebastian's home address in a half hour. Start with osetra caviar and whatever you can find that's close to… Hang on." He looked to Sarah. "What was that again?"

"Fiambre."

"Fiambre. It's a salad…Hell, I don't know…Right. Right. Half an hour."

Sarah was staring at him when he cut the connection. "Who was that?"

"My executive assistant."

"She's here, in New York?"

"It's a he. Patrick Donovan. We used to fly together. He's back in L.A."

"And he's going to have champagne and caviar delivered to our apartment in half an hour?"

"That's why he gets paid the big bucks." He nodded to the phone she clutched in her hand. "You better call the duchess. With all this traffic, lunch will probably get there before we do."

Despite his advance preparations, Dev had to shake off a serious case of nerves when he and Sarah stepped out of the elevator at the Dakota. His introduction to Charlotte St. Sebastian last night had given him a keen appreciation of both her intellect and her fierce devotion to her granddaughters. He had no idea how she'd react to this sudden engagement, but he suspected she'd make him sweat.

Sarah obviously suspected the same thing. She paused at the door to their apartment, key in hand, and gave him a look that was half challenge, half anxious appeal.

"She…she has a heart condition. We need to be careful how we orchestrate this."

"I'll follow your lead."

Pulling in a deep breath, she squared her shoulders. The key rattled in the lock, and the door opened on a parade of white-jacketed waiters just about to exit the apartment. Their arms full of empty cartons, they stepped aside.

"Your grandmother told us to set up in the dining room," the waiter in charge informed Sarah. "And may I say, ma'am, she has exquisite taste in crystal. Bohemian, isn't it?"

"Yes, it is."

"I thought so. No other lead crystal has that thin, liquid sheen."

Nodding, Sarah hurried down the hall. Dev lingered to add a hefty tip to the service fee he knew Patrick would have already taken care of. Gushing their thanks, the team departed and Dev made his way to the duchess's high-ceilinged dining room.

He paused on the threshold to survey the scene. The mahogany table could easily seat twelve, probably twenty or more with leaves in, but had been set with four places at the far end. Bone-white china gleamed. An impressive array of ruby-red goblets sparkled at each place setting. A sideboard held a row of domed silver serving dishes, and an opened bottle of champagne sat in a silver ice bucket.

Damn! Patrick would insist Dev add another zero to his already astronomical salary for pulling this one off.

"I presume this is your doing, Devon."

His glance zinged to the duchess. She stood ramrod straight at the head of the table, her hands folded one atop the other on the ivory handle of her cane. The housekeeper, Maria, hovered just behind her.

"Yes, ma'am."

"I also presume you're going to tell me the reason for this impromptu celebration."

Having agreed to let Sarah take the lead, Dev merely moved to her side and eased an arm around her waist. She stiffened, caught herself almost instantly and relaxed.

"We have two reasons to celebrate, Grandmama. Dev's asked me to go to Paris with him."

"So I understand. Maria informed me you asked her to stay with me while you're gone."

Her arctic tone left no doubt as to her feelings about the matter.

"It's just for a short while, and more for me than for you. This way I won't feel so bad about rushing off and leaving you on such short notice."

The duchess didn't unbend. If anything, her arthritic fingers clutched the head of her cane more tightly.

"And the second reason for this celebration?"

Sarah braced herself. Dev could feel her body go taut against his while she struggled to frame their agreement in terms her grandmother would accept. It was time for him to step in and draw the duchess's fire.

"My sisters will tell you I'm seriously deficient in the romance department, ma'am. They'll also tell you I tend to bulldoze over any and all obstacles when I set my sights on something. Sarah put up a good fight, but I convinced her we should get engaged before we take off for Paris."

"Madre de Dios!" The exclamation burst from Maria, who gaped at Sarah. "You are *engaged*? To this man?"

When she nodded, the duchess's chin shot up. Her glance skewered Dev where he stood. In contrast to her stark silence, Maria gave quick, joyous thanks to the Virgin Mary while making the sign of the cross three times in rapid succession.

"How I prayed for this, *chica!*"

Tears sparkling in her brown eyes, she rushed over to crush Sarah against her generous bosom. Dev didn't get a hug, but he was hauled down by his lapels and treated to a hearty kiss on both cheeks.

The duchess remained standing where she was. Dev was damned if he could read her expression. When Sarah approached, Charlotte's narrow-eyed stare shifted to her granddaughter.

"We stopped by Cartier on our way here, Grandmama. Dev wanted to buy me an engagement ring."

She raised her left hand, and the effect on the duchess was instant and electric.

"Dear God! Is that…? Is that the Russian Rose?"

"Yes," Sarah said gently.

Charlotte reached out a veined hand and stroked the emerald's rounded surface with a shaking fingertip. Dev felt uncomfortably like a voyeur as he watched a succession of naked emotions cross the older woman's face. For a long moment, she was in another time, another place, reliving memories that obviously brought both great joy and infinite sadness.

With an effort that was almost painful to observe, she returned to the present and smiled at Sarah.

"Your grandfather gave me the Rose for my eighteenth birthday. I always intended you to have it."

Her glance shifted once again to Dev. Something passed between them, but before he could figure out just what the hell it was, the duchess became all brisk efficiency.

"Well, Sarah, since you're traipsing off to Paris on such short notice, I think we should sample this sumptuous feast your…your fiancé has so generously arranged. Then you'll have to pack. Devon, will you pour the champagne?"

"Yes, ma'am."

Dev's misguided belief that he'd escaped unscathed lasted only until they'd finished brunch and Sarah went to pack. He got up to help Maria clear the table. She waved him back to his seat.

"I will do this. You sit and keep *la duquesa* company."

The moment Maria bustled through the door to the kitchen, *la duquesa* let loose with both barrels. Her pale eyes dangerous, she unhooked her cane from her chair arm and stabbed it at Dev like a sword.

"Let's be sure we understand each other, Mr. Hunter. I

may have been forced to sell the Russian Rose, but if you've purchased it with the mistaken idea you can also purchase my granddaughter, you'd best think again. One can't buy class or good genes. One either has both—" she jabbed his chest with the cane for emphasis "—or one doesn't."

Geesh! Good thing he was facing this woman over three feet of ebony and not down the barrel of an M16. Dev didn't doubt she'd pull the trigger if he answered wrong.

"First," he replied, "I had no idea that emerald once belonged to you. Second, I'm perfectly satisfied with my genes. Third…"

He stopped to think about that one. His feelings for Sarah St. Sebastian had become too confused, too fast. The way she moved…. The smile in her green eyes when she let down her guard for a few moments…. Her fierce loyalty to her grandmother and ditz of a sister…. Everything about her seemed to trigger both heat and hunger.

"Third," he finally admitted, "there's no way I'll ever match Sarah's style or elegance. All I can do is appreciate it, which I most certainly do."

The duchess kept her thoughts hidden behind her narrowed eyes for several moments. Then she dropped the tip of the cane and thumped the floor.

"Very well. I'll wait to see how matters develop."

She eased back against her chair and Dev started to breathe again.

"I'm sure you're aware," she said into the tentative truce, "that Paris is one of Sarah's favorite cities?"

"We haven't gotten around to sharing all our favorites yet," he replied with perfect truthfulness. "I do know she attended the Sorbonne for a year as an undergraduate."

That much was in the background dossier, as was the fact she'd majored in art history. Dev planned to use whatever spare time they might have in Paris to hit a few museums with her. He looked forward to exploring the Louvre or the Cluny with someone who shared his burgeoning interest in art. He was certainly no expert, but his appreciation of art in its various forms had grown with each incremental increase in his personal income…as evidenced by the Byzantine medallion.

The belated reminder of why he was here, being poked in the chest by this imperious, indomitable woman, hit with a belated punch. He'd let the side details of his "engagement" momentarily obscure the fact that he'd arm-twisted Sarah into it. He was using her, ruthlessly and with cold deliberation, as a tool to help close an important deal. Once that deal was closed…

To borrow the duchess's own words, Dev decided, they'd just have to wait and see how matters develop. He wouldn't employ the same ruthlessness and calculation to seduce the eminently seductive Lady Sarah as he had to get a ring on her finger. But neither would he pass up the chance to finesse her into bed if the opportunity offered.

The possibility sent a spear of heat into his belly. With a sheer effort of will, he gave the indomitable Charlotte St. Sebastian no sign of the knee-jerk reaction. But he had to admit he was now looking forward to this trip with considerably more anticipation than when Jean-Jacques Girault first requested it.

Seven

Three hours out over the Atlantic Sarah had yet to get past her surprise.

"I still can't believe Grandmama took it so well," she said, her fingers poised over the keyboard of her laptop. "Not just the engagement. This trip to Paris. The hefty bonus you're paying Maria. Everything!"

Dev looked up from the text message he'd just received. Their first-class seat pods were separated by a serving console holding his scotch, her wine and a tray of appetizers, but they were seated close enough for him to see the lingering disbelief in her jade-green eyes.

"Why shouldn't she take it well?" he countered. "She grilled me last night about my parents, my grandparents, my siblings, my education, my health, my club memberships and my bank account. She squeezed everything else she wanted to know out of me today at lunch. It was a close call, but evidently I passed muster."

"I think it was the ring," Sarah murmured, her gaze on the milky stone that crowned her finger. "Her whole attitude changed when she spotted it."

Dev knew damn well it was the ring, and noted with

interest the guilt and embarrassment tinging his fiancée's cheeks.

"I supposed I should have told you at Cartier that the Russian Rose once belonged to Grandmama."

"Not a problem. I'm just glad it was available."

She was quiet for a moment, still pondering the luncheon.

"Do you know what I find so strange? Grandmama didn't once ask how we could have fallen in love so quickly."

"Maybe because she comes from a different era. Plus, she went through some really rough times. Could be your security weighs as heavily in her mind as your happiness."

"That can't be it. She's always told Gina and me that her marriage was a love match. She had to defy her parents to make it happen."

"Yes, but look what came next," Dev said gently. "From what I've read, the Soviet takeover of her country was brutal. She witnessed your grandfather's execution. She barely escaped the same fate and had to make a new life for herself and her baby in a different country."

Sarah fingered the emerald, her profile etched with sadness. "Then she lost my parents and got stuck with Gina and me."

"Why do I think she didn't regard it as getting stuck? I suspect you and your sister went a long way to filling the hole in her heart."

"Gina more than me."

"I doubt that," Dev drawled.

As he'd anticipated, she jumped instantly to her sister's defense.

"I know you think Gina's a total airhead..."

"I do."

"...but she's so full of joy and life that no one—I repeat, *no one*—can be in her company for more than three minutes without cracking a smile."

Her eyes fired lethal darts, daring him to disagree. He didn't have to. He'd achieved his objective and erased the sad memories. Rather than risk alienating her, he changed the subject.

"I just got a text from Monsieur Girault. He says he's delighted you were able to get away and accompany me."

"Really?" Sarah hiked a politely skeptical brow. "What does his wife say?"

To Dev's chagrin, heat crawled up his neck. He'd flown in and out of a dozen different combat zones, for God's sake! Could stare down union presidents and corporate sharks with equal skill. Yet Elise Girault had thrown him completely off stride when he'd bent to give her the obligatory kiss on both cheeks. Her whispered suggestion was so startling—and so erotic—he'd damned near gotten whiplash when he'd jerked his head back. Then she'd let loose with a booming, raucous laugh that invited him to share in their private joke.

"He didn't say," Dev said in answer to Sarah's question, "but he did ask what you would like to do while we're locked up in a conference room. He indicated his wife is a world-class shopper. Apparently she's well-known at most of the high-end boutiques."

He realized his mistake the moment the words were out. He'd run Sarah St. Sebastian's financials. He knew how strapped she was.

"That reminds me," he said with deliberate nonchalance. "I don't intend for you to incur any out-of-pocket expenses as part of our deal. There'll be a credit card waiting for you at the hotel."

"Please tell me you're kidding."

Her reaction shouldn't have surprised him. Regal elegance was only one of the traits Lady Sarah had inherited from her grandmother. Stiff-necked pride had to rank right up near the top of the list.

"Be reasonable, Sarah. You're providing me a personal service."

Which was becoming more personal by the hour. Dev was getting used to her stimulating company. The heat she ignited in him still took him by surprise, though. He hadn't figured that into his plan.

"Of course I'll cover your expenses."

Her expression turned glacial. "The hotel, yes. Any meals we take with Madame and Monsieur Girault, yes. A shopping spree on the rue du Faubourg Saint-Honoré, no."

"Fine. It's your call."

He tried to recover with an admiring survey of her petal-pink dress. The fabric was thick and satiny, the cut sleek. A coat in the same style hung in their cabin's private closet.

"The rue du Whatever has nothing on Fifth Avenue. That classy New York look will have Elise Girault demanding an immediate trip to the States."

She stared at him blankly for a moment, then burst into laughter. "You're not real up on haute couture, are you?"

"Any of my sisters would tell you I don't know haute from hamburger."

"I wouldn't go that far," she said, still chuckling. "Unless I miss my guess, your shoes are Moroccan leather, the suit's hand-tailored and the tie comes from a little shop just off the Grand Canal in Venice."

"Damn, you're good! Although Patrick tells me he orders the ties from Milan, not Venice. So where did that dress come from?"

"It's vintage Balenciaga. Grandmama bought it in Madrid decades ago."

The smile remained, but Dev thought it dimmed a few degrees.

"She disposed of most of her designer originals when… when they went out of style, but she kept enough to provide a treasure trove for me. Thank goodness! Retro is the new 'new,' you know. I'm the envy of everyone at *Beguile*."

Dev could read behind the lines. The duchess must have sold off her wardrobe as well as her jewelry over the years. It was miracle she'd managed to hang on to the apartment at the Dakota. The thought of what the duchess and Sarah had gone through kicked Dev's admiration for them both up another notch. Also, his determination to treat Sarah to something new and obscenely expensive. He knew better than to step on her pride again, though, and said merely, "Retro looks good on you."

"Thank you."

After what passed for the airline's gourmet meal, Dev used his in-flight wireless connection to crunch numbers for his meetings with Girault and company while Sarah went back to work on her laptop. She'd promised Alexis she would finish the layout for the Summer Sea-escapes but the perspectives just wouldn't gel. After juggling Martha's Vineyard with Catalina Island and South Padre Island with South Georgia Island, she decided she would have to swing by *Beguile*'s Paris offices to see how the layout looked on a twenty-five-inch monitor before shooting it off to Alexis for review.

Dev was still crunching numbers when she folded down the lid of her computer. With a polite good-night, she tugged up the airline's fleecy blue blanket and curled into her pod.

A gentle nudge brought her awake some hours later. She blinked gritty eyes and decided reality was more of a fantasy than her dreams. Dev had that bad-boy look again. Tie loosened. Shirt collar open. Dark circles below his blue eyes.

"We'll be landing in less than an hour," he told her.

As if to emphasize the point, a flight attendant appeared with a pot of fresh-brewed coffee. Sarah gulped down a half cup before she took the amenity kit provided to all business- and first-class passengers to the lavatory. She emerged with her face washed, teeth brushed, hair combed and her soul ready for the magic that was springtime in Paris.

Or the magic that might have been.

Spring hadn't yet made it to northern France. The temperature hovered around fifty, and a cold rain was coming down in sheets when Sarah and Dev emerged from the terminal and ducked into a waiting limo. The trees lining the roads from the airport showed only a hint of new green and the fields were brown and sere.

Once inside the city, Paris's customary snarl of traffic engulfed them. Neither the traffic nor the nasty weather could dim the glory of the 7th arrondissement, however. The townhomes and ministries, once the residences of France's wealthiest nobility, displayed their mansard roofs and wrought-iron balconies with haughty disregard for the pelting rain. Sarah caught glimpses of the Eiffel Tower's iron symmetry before the limo rolled to a stop on a quiet side street in the heart of Saint-Germain. Surprise brought her around in her seat to face Dev.

"We're staying at the Hôtel Verneuil?"

"We are."

"Gina and I and Grandmama stayed here years ago, on our last trip abroad together."

"So the duchess informed me." His mouth curved. "She also informed me that I'm to take you to Café Michaud to properly celebrate our engagement," he said with a smile.

Sarah fell a little bit in love with him at that moment. Not because he'd booked them into this small gem of a palace instead of a suite at the much larger and far more expensive Crillon or George V. Because he'd made such an effort with her grandmother.

Surprised and shaken by the warmth that curled around her heart, she tried to recover as they exited the limo. "From what I remember, the Verneuil only has twenty-five or twenty-six rooms. The hotel's usually full. I'm surprised you could get us in with such short notice."

"I didn't. Patrick did. After which he informed me that I'd just doubled his Christmas bonus."

"I have to meet this man."

"That can be arranged."

He said it with a casualness that almost hid the implication behind his promise. Sarah caught it, however. The careless words implied a future beyond Paris.

She wasn't ready to think about that. Instead she looked around the lobby while Dev went to the reception desk. The exposed beams, rich tapestries and heavy furniture covered in red velvet hadn't changed since her last visit ten or twelve years ago. Apparently the management hadn't, either. The receptionist must have buzzed her boss. He emerged from the back office, his shoulders stooped beneath his formal morning coat and a wide smile on his face.

"*Bonjour,* Lady Sarah!"

A quick glance at his name tag provided his name. "*Bonjour,* Monsieur LeBon."

"What a delight to have you stay with us again," he exclaimed in French, the Parisian accent so different from that of the provinces. "How is the duchess?"

"She's very well, thank you."

"I'm told this trip is in honor of a special occasion," the manager beamed. "May I offer you my most sincere congratulations?"

"Thank you," she said again, trying not to cringe at the continuation of their deception.

LeBon switched to English to offer his felicitations to Dev. "If I may be so bold to say it, Monsieur Hunter, you are a very lucky man to have captured the heart of one such as Lady Sarah."

"Extremely lucky," Dev agreed.

"Allow me to show you to your floor."

He pushed the button to summon the elevator, then stood aside for them to enter the brass-bedecked cage. While it lifted them to the upper floors, he apologized profusely for not being able to give them adjoining rooms as had been requested.

"We moved several of our guests as your so very capable assistant suggested, Monsieur Hunter, and have put you and Lady Sarah in chambers only a short distance apart. I hope they will be satisfactory."

Sarah's was more than satisfactory. A mix of antique, marble and modern, it offered a four-poster bed and a lovely sitting area with a working fireplace and a tiny balcony. But it was the view from the balcony that delighted her artist's soul.

The rain had softened to a drizzle. It glistened on the slate-gray rooftops of Paris. Endless rows of chimneys rose from the roofs like sentries standing guard over their city. And in the distance were the twin Gothic towers and flying buttresses of Notre Dame.

"I don't have anything scheduled until three this afternoon," Dev said while Monsieur LeBon waited to escort him to his own room. "Would you like to rest awhile, then go out for lunch?"

The city beckoned, and Sarah ached to answer its call. "I'm not tired. I think I'd like to take a walk."

"In the rain?"

"That's when Paris is at its best. The streets, the cafés, seem to steal the light. Everything shimmers."

"Okay," Dev said, laughing, "you've convinced me. I'll change and rap on your door in, say, fifteen minutes?"

"Oh, but…"

She stopped just short of blurting out that she hadn't intended that as an invitation. She could hardly say she didn't want her fiancé's company with Monsieur LeBon beaming his approval of a romantic stroll.

"…I'll need a bit more time than that," she finished. "Let's say thirty minutes."

"A half hour it is."

As she changed into lightweight wool slacks and a hip-length, cherry-red sweater coat that belted at the waist, Sarah tried to analyze her reluctance to share these first hours in Paris with Dev. She suspected it stemmed from the emotion that had welled up when they'd first pulled up at the Hôtel Verneuil. She knew then that she could fall for him, and fall hard. What worried her was that it wouldn't take very much to push her over the precipice.

True, he'd blackmailed her into this uncomfortable charade. Also true, he'd put a ring on her finger and hustled her onto a plane before she could formulate a coherent protest. In the midst of those autocratic acts, though, he'd shown incredible forbearance and generosity.

Then there were the touches, the kisses, the ridiculous whoosh every time he smiled at her. Devon Hunter had made *Beguile*'s list based on raw sex appeal. Sarah now realized he possessed something far more potent…and more dangerous to her peace of mind.

She had to remember this was a short-term assignment. Dev had stipulated it would last only until he wrapped up negotiations on his big deal. It looked now as though that might happen within the next few days. Then this would all be over.

The thought didn't depress her. Sarah wouldn't let it. But worked hard to keep the thought at bay.

She was ready when Dev knocked. Wrapping on a biscuit-colored rain cape, she tossed one of its flaps over a shoulder on her way to the door. With her hair tucked up under a flat-brimmed Dutch-boy cap, she was rainproof and windproof.

"Nice hat," Dev said when she stepped into the hall.

"Thanks."

"Nice everything, actually."

She could have said the same. This was the first time she'd seen him in anything other than a suit. The man was made for jeans. Or vice versa. Their snug fit emphasized his flat belly and lean flanks. And, she added with a gulp when he turned to press the button for the elevator, his tight, trim butt.

He'd added a cashmere scarf in gray-and-blue plaid to his leather bomber jacket, but hadn't bothered with a hat. Sarah worried that it would be too cold for him, but when they exited the hotel, they found the rain was down to a fine mist and the temperature had climbed a few degrees.

Dev took her arm as they crossed the street, then tucked it in his as they started down the boulevard. Sarah felt awkward with that arrangement at first. Elbow to elbow, shoulder to shoulder, strolling along the rain-washed boulevard, they looked like the couple they weren't.

Gradually, Sarah got used to the feel of him beside her, to the way he matched his stride to hers. And bit by bit, the magic of Paris eased her nagging sense that this was all just a charade.

Even this late in the morning the *boulangeries* still emitted their seductive, tantalizing scent of fresh-baked bread. Baguettes sprouted from tall baskets and the racks were crammed with braided loaves. The pastry shops, too, had set out their day's wares. The exquisitely crafted sweets, tarts, chocolate éclairs, gâteaux, caramel mousse, napoleons, macaroons—all were true works of art, and completely impossible to resist.

"God, these look good," Dev murmured, his gaze on the colorful display. "Are you up for a coffee and an éclair?"

"Always. But my favorite patisserie in all Paris is just a couple of blocks away. Can you hold out a little longer?"

"I'll try," he said, assuming an expression of heroic resolution.

Laughing, Sarah pressed his arm closer to her side and guided him the few blocks. The tiny patisserie was nested between a bookstore and a bank. Three dime-size wrought-iron tables sat under the striped awning out front; three more were wedged inside. Luckily two women were getting up from one of the tables when Dev and Sarah entered.

Sarah ordered an espresso and *tart au citron* for herself, and a café au lait for Dev, then left him debating his choice of pastries while she claimed the table. She loosed the flaps of her cape and let it drift over the back of her chair while she observed the drama taking place at the pastry case.

With no other customers waiting, the young woman behind the counter inspected Dev with wide eyes while he checked out the colorful offerings. When he made his selection, she slid the pastry onto a plate and offered it with a question.

"You are American?"

He flashed her a friendly smile. "I am."

Sarah guessed what was coming even before the woman's face lit up with eager recognition.

"Aah, I knew it. You are Number Three, yes?"

Dev's smile tipped into a groan, but he held his cool as she called excitedly to her coworkers.

"C'est lui! C'est lui! Monsieur Hunter. Numéro trois."

Sarah bit her lip as a small bevy of females in white aprons converged at the counter. Dev took the fuss with good grace and even autographed a couple of paper napkins before retreating to the table with his chocolate éclair.

Sarah felt the urge to apologize but merely nodded when he asked grimly if *Beguile* had a wide circulation in France.

"It's our third-largest market."

"Great."

He stabbed his éclair and had to dig deep for a smile when the server delivered their coffees.

"In fact," Sarah said after the girl giggled and departed,

"*Beguile* has an office here in the city. I was going to swing by there when you go for your meeting."

"I'll arrange a car for you."

The reply was polite, but perfunctory. The enchantment of their stroll through Paris's rain-washed streets had dissipated with the mist.

"No need. I'll take the subway."

"Your call," Dev replied. "I'll contact you later and let you know what time we're meeting the Giraults for dinner tonight."

Eight

The French offices of *Beguile* were located only a few blocks from the Arc de Triomphe, on rue Balzac. Sarah always wondered what that famed French novelist and keen observer of human absurdities would think of a glossy publication that pandered to so many of those absurdities.

The receptionist charged with keeping the masses at bay glanced up from her desk with a polite expression that morphed into a welcoming smile when she spotted Sarah.

"*Bonjour,* Sarah! So good to see you again!"

"*Bonjour,* Madeline. Good to see you, too. How are the twins?"

"Horrors," the receptionist replied with a half laugh, half groan. "Absolute horrors. Here are their latest pictures."

After duly admiring the impish-looking three-year-olds, Sarah rounded the receptionist's desk and walked a corridor lined with framed, poster-size copies of *Beguile* covers. Paul Vincent, the senior editor, was pacing his glass cage of an office and using both hands to emphasize whatever point he was trying to make to the person on the speakerphone. Sarah tipped him a wave and would have proceeded to the production unit, but Paul gestured her inside and abruptly terminated his call.

"Sarah!"

Grasping her hands, he kissed her on both cheeks. She bent just a bit so he could hit the mark. At five-four, Paul tended to be as sensitive about his height as he was about the kidney-shaped birthmark discoloring a good portion of his jaw. Yet despite what he called his little imperfections, his unerring eye for color and style had propelled him from the designers' cutting rooms to his present exalted position.

"Alexis emailed to say you would be in Paris," he informed Sarah. "She's instructed me to put François and his crew at your complete disposal."

"For what?"

"To take photos of you and your fiancé. She wants all candids, no posed shots and plenty of romantic backdrop in both shallow and distant depth of field. François says he'll use wide aperture at the Eiffel Tower, perhaps F2.8 to…"

"No, Paul."

"No F2.8? Well, you'll have to speak with François about that."

"No, Paul. No wide aperture, no candids, no Eiffel Tower, no François!"

"But Alexis…."

"Wants to capitalize on my engagement to Number Three. Yes, I know. My fiancé agreed to a photo shoot in New York, but that's as far as either he or I will go. We told Alexis that before we left."

"Then you had better tell her again."

"I will," she said grimly. "In the meantime, I need to use Production's monitors to take a last look at the layout I've been working on. When I zap it to Alexis, I'll remind her of our agreement."

She turned to leave, but Paul stopped her. "What can you tell me of the Chicago meeting?"

The odd inflection in his voice gave Sarah pause. Wondering what was behind it, she searched her mind. So much had happened in the past few days that she'd forgotten about the shuttle Alexis had jumped for an unscheduled meeting with the head of their publishing group. All she'd thought about her boss's unscheduled absence at the time was that it had provided a short reprieve. Paul's question now brought the Chicago meeting forcibly to mind.

"I can't tell you anything," she said honestly. "I didn't have a chance to talk to Alexis about it before I left. Why, what have you heard?"

He folded his arms, bent an elbow and tapped two fingers against the birthmark on his chin. It was a nervous gesture, one he rarely allowed. That he would give in to it now generated a distinct unease in Sarah.

"I've heard rumors," he admitted. "Only rumors, you understand."

"What rumors?"

The fingers picked up speed, machine-gunning his chin.

"Some say... Not me, I assure you! But some say that Alexis is too old. Too out of touch with our target readership. Some say the romance has gone out of her, and out of our magazine. Before, we used to beguile, to tantalize. Now we titillate."

Much to her chagrin, Sarah couldn't argue the point. The butt shot of Dev that Alexis had insisted on was case in point. In the most secret corners of her heart, she agreed with the ambiguous, unnamed "some" Paul referenced.

Despite her frequent differences of opinion with her boss, however, she owed Alexis her loyalty and support. She'd hired Sarah right out of college, sans experience, sans credentials. Grandmama might insist Sarah's title had influenced that decision. Maybe so, but the title hadn't done more than get a neophyte's foot in the door. She'd sweated blood to work her way up to layout editor. And now, apparently, it was payback time.

Alexis confirmed that some time later in her response to Sarah's email.

Sea-escapes layout looks good. We'll go with it. Please re-think the Paris photo shoot. Chicago feels we need more romance in our mag. You and Hunter personify that, at least as far as our readers are concerned.

The email nagged at Sarah all afternoon. She used the remainder of her private time to wander through her favorite museum, but not even the Musée d'Orsay could resolve her moral dilemma. Questions came at her, dive-bombing like suicidal mosquitoes as she strolled through the converted railroad station that now housed some of the world's most celebrated works of art.

All but oblivious to the Matisses and Rodins, she weighed her options. Should she support her boss or accede to Dev's demand for privacy? What about the mess with Gina? Would Alexis exploit that, too, if pushed to the wall? Would she play up the elder sister's engagement as a desperate attempt to save the younger from a charge of larceny?

She would. Sarah knew damned well she would. The certainty curdled like sour milk in the pit of her stomach. Whom did she most owe her loyalty to? Gina? Dev? Alexis? Herself?

The last thought was so heretical it gnawed at Sarah's insides while she prepped for her first meeting with the Giraults early that evening. Dev had told her this would be an informal dinner at the couple's Paris town house.

"Ha!" she muttered as she added a touch of mascara. "I'll bet it's informal."

Going with instinct, she opted for a hip-length tuxedo jacket that had been one of Grandmama's favorite pieces. Sarah had extracted the jacket from the to-be-sold pile on at least three separate occasions. Vintage was vintage, but

Louis Féraud was art. He'd opened his first house of fashion in Cannes 1950, became one of Brigitte Bardot's favorite designers and grew into a legend in his own lifetime.

This jacket was quintessential Féraud. The contour-hugging design featured wide satin lapels and a double-breasted, two-button front fastening. Sarah paired it with a black, lace-edged chemise and wide-pegged black satin pants. A honey-colored silk handkerchief peeked from the breast pocket. A thin gold bangle circled her wrist. With her hair swept up in a smooth twist, she looked restrained and refined.

For some reason, though, restrained just didn't hack it tonight. Not while she was playing tug-of-war between fiercely conflicting loyalties. She wanted to do right by Dev. And Alexis. And Gina. And herself. Elise Girault could take a flying leap.

Frowning, she unclipped her hair and let the dark mass swirl to her shoulders. Then she slipped out of the jacket and tugged off the chemise. When she pulled the jacket on again, the two-button front dipped dangerously low. Grandmama would have a cow if she saw how much shadowy cleavage her Sarah now displayed. Dev, she suspected, would approve.

He did. Instantly and enthusiastically. Bending an arm against the doorjamb, he gave a long, low whistle.

"You look fantastic."

"Thanks." Honesty compelled her to add, "So do you."

If the afternoon negotiating session with Monsieur Girault had produced any stress, it didn't show in his face. He was clean shaven, clear eyed and smelled so darned good Sarah almost leaned in for a deeper whiff. His black hair still gleamed with damp. From a shower, she wondered as she fought the urged to feather her fingers through it, or the foggy drizzle that had kept up all day?

His suit certainly wasn't vintage, but had obviously been

tailored with the same loving skill as Grandmama's jacket. With it he wore a crisp blue shirt topped by a blue-and-silver-striped tie.

"What was it Oscar Wilde said about ties?" Sarah murmured, eyeing the expensive neckwear.

"Beats me."

"Something about a well-tied tie being the first serious step in a man's life. Of course, that was back when it took them hours to achieve the perfect crease in their cravat."

"Glad those days are gone. Speaking of gone… The car's waiting." He bowed and swept a hand toward the door. "Shall we go, *ma chérie?*"

Her look of surprise brought a smug grin.

"I had some time after my meeting so I pulled up a few phrases on Google Translate. How's the accent?"

"Well…"

"That bad, huh?"

"I've heard worse."

But not much worse. Hiding a smile, she picked up her clutch and led the way to the door.

"How did the meeting go, by the way?"

"We're making progress. Enough that my chief of production and a team of our corporate attorneys are in the air as we speak. We still need to hammer out a few details, but we're close."

"You *must* be making progress if you're bringing in a whole team."

Sarah refused to acknowledge the twinge that gave her. She hadn't really expected to share much of Paris with Dev. He was here on business. And she was here to make sure that business didn't get derailed by the wife of his prospective partner. She reminded herself of that fact as the limo glided through the lamp-lit streets.

Jean-Jacques Girault and his wife greeted them at the door to their magnificent town house. Once inside the palatial foyer, the two couples engaged in the obligatory cheek-kissing. Madame Girault behaved herself as she congratulated her guests on their engagement, but Dev stuck close to his fiancée just in case.

The exchange gave Sarah time to assess her hostess. The blonde had to be in her mid-fifties, but she had the lithe build and graceful carriage of a ballerina…which she used to be, she informed Sarah with a nod toward the portrait holding place of honor in the palatial foyer. The larger-than-life-size oil depicted a much younger Elise Girault costumed as Odile, the evil black swan in Tchaikovsky's *Swan Lake.*

"I loved dancing that part." With a smile as wicked as the one she wore in the portrait, Madame Girault hooked an arm in Sarah's and led her through a set of open double doors into a high-ceilinged salon. "Being bad is so much more fun than being good, yes?"

"Unless, as happens to Odile in some versions of *Swan Lake,* being bad gets you an arrow through the heart."

The older woman's laugh burst out, as loud and booming as a cannon. "Aha! You are warning me, I think, to keep my hands off your so-handsome Devon."

"If the ballet slipper fits…"

Her laugh foghorned again, noisy and raucous and totally infectious. Sarah found herself grinning as Madame Girault spoke over her shoulder.

"I like her, Devon."

She pronounced it Dee-vón, with the accent on the last syllable.

"I was prepared not to, you understand, as I want you for myself. Perhaps we can arrange a ménage à trois, yes?"

With her back to Dev, Sarah missed his reaction to the suggestion. She would have bet it wasn't as benign as Monsieur Girault's.

"Elise, my pet. You'll shock our guests with these little jokes of yours."

The look his wife gave Sarah brimmed with mischief and the unmistakable message that she was *not* joking.

Much to Sarah's surprise, she enjoyed the evening. Elise Girault didn't try to be anything but herself. She was at times sophisticated, at other times outrageous, but she didn't cross the line Sarah had drawn in the sand. Or in this case, in the near-priceless nineteenth-century Aubusson carpet woven in green-and-gold florals.

The Giraults and their guests took cocktails in the salon and dinner in an exquisitely paneled dining room with windows overlooking the Seine. The lively conversation ranged from their hostess's years at the Ballet de l'Opéra de Paris to Sarah's work at *Beguile* to, inevitably, the megabusiness of aircraft manufacturing. The glimpse into a world she'd had no previous exposure to fascinated Sarah, but Elise tolerated it only until the last course was cleared.

"Enough, Jean-Jacques!"

Pushing away from the table, she rose. Her husband and guests followed suit.

"We will take coffee and dessert in the petite salon. And you," she said, claiming Dev's arm, "will tell me what convinced this delightful woman to marry you. It was the story in *Beguile,* yes?" Her wicked smile returning, she threw Sarah an arch look. "The truth, now. Is his derriere as delicious as it looked in your magazine?"

Her husband shook his head. "Be good, Elise."

"I am, *mon cher.* Sooo good."

"I'm good, Dee-vón." Grinning, Sarah batted her lashes as the Hôtel Verneuil's elevator whisked them upward. "Sooo good."

Amused, Dev folded his arms and leaned his shoulders against the cage. She wasn't tipsy—she'd restricted her alcoholic intake to one aperitif, a single glass of wine and a few sips of brandy—but she was looser than he'd yet seen her.

He liked her this way. Her green eyes sparkling. Her hair windblown and brushing her shoulders. Her tuxedo jacket providing intermittent and thoroughly tantalizing glimpses of creamy breasts.

Liked, hell. He wanted to devour her whole.

"You were certainly good tonight," he agreed. "Especially when Elise tried to pump you for details about our sex life. I still don't know how you managed to give the impression of torrid heat when all you did was arch a brow."

"Ah, yes. The regal lift. It's one of Grandmama's best weapons, along with the chin tilt and the small sniff."

She demonstrated all three and had him grinning while he walked her to her door.

"Elise may be harder to fend off when she and I have lunch tomorrow," Sarah warned as she extracted the key card from her purse. "I may need to improvise."

His pulse jumping, Dev took the key and slid it into the electronic lock. The lock snicked, the door opened and he made his move.

"No reason you should have to improvise."

She turned, her expression at once wary and disbelieving. "Are you suggesting we go to bed together to satisfy Elise Girault's prurient curiosity?"

"No, ma'am." He bent and brushed his lips across hers. "I'm suggesting we go to bed together to satisfy ours."

Her jaw sagged. "You're kidding, right?"

"No, ma'am," he said again, half laughing, wholly serious.

She snapped her mouth shut, but the fact that she didn't stalk inside and slam the door in his face set Dev's pulse jumping again.

"Maybe," she said slowly, her eyes locked with his, "we could go a little way down that road. Just far enough to provide Elise with a few juicy details."

That was all the invitation he needed. Scooping her into his arms, he strode into the room and kicked the door shut. The maid had left the lamps on and turned down the duvet on the bed. Much as Dev ached to vector in that direction, he aimed for the sofa instead. He settled on its plush cushions with Sarah in his lap.

Exerting fierce control, he slid a palm under the silky splash of her hair. Her nape was warm, her lips parted, her gaze steady. The thought flashed into Dev's mind that he was already pretty far down the road.

Rock hard and hurting, he bent his head again. No mere brush of lips this time. No tentative exploration. No show for the cameras. This was hunger, raw and hot. He tried to throttle it back, but Sarah sabotaged that effort by matching him kiss for kiss, touch for touch. His fingers speared through her hair. Hers traced the line of his jaw, slipped inside his collar, found the knot of his tie.

"To hell with Oscar Wilde," she muttered after a moment. "The tie has to go."

The tie went. So did the suit coat. When she popped the top two buttons of his dress shirt, he reached for the ones on her jacket. The first one slid through its opening and Dev saw she wasn't wearing a bra. With a fervent prayer of thanks, he fingered the second button.

"I've been fantasizing about doing this from the moment you opened the door to me this evening," he admitted, his voice rough.

"I fantasized about it, too. Must be why I discarded the chemise I usually wear with this outfit."

Her honesty shot straight to his heart. She didn't play games. Didn't tease or go all pouty and coy. She was as hungry as Dev and not ashamed to show it.

Aching with need, he slid the second button through its opening. The satin lapels gaped open, baring her breasts. They were small and proud and tipped with dark rose nipples that Dev couldn't even begin to resist. Hefting her a little higher, he trailed a line of kisses down one slope and caught a nipple between his lips.

Her neck arched. Her head tipped back. With a small groan, Sarah reveled in the sensations that streaked from her breast to her belly. They were so deep, so intense, she purred with pleasure.

It took her a few moments to realize she wasn't actually emitting that low, humming sound. It was coming from the clutch purse she'd dropped on the sofa table.

"That's my cell phone," she panted through waves of pleasure. "I put it on vibrate at the Giraults."

"Ignore it."

Dev turned his attention to her other breast and Sarah was tempted, so tempted, to follow his gruff instruction.

"I can't," she groaned. "It could be Grandmama. Or Maria," she added with a little clutch of panic.

She scrambled upright and grabbed her bag. A glance at the face associated in her address book with the incoming number made her sag with relief.

Only for a moment, however. What could Alexis want, calling this late? Remembering her conversation with Paul Vincent at *Beguile*'s Paris office this afternoon, Sarah once again felt the tug of conflicting loyalties.

"Sarah? Are you there?" Alexis's hoarse rasp rattled through voice mail. "Pick up if you are."

Sarah sent Dev an apologetic glance and hit Answer. "I'm here, Alexis."

"Sorry, kiddo, I didn't think about the time difference. Were you in bed?"

"Almost," Dev muttered.

Sarah made a shushing motion with her free hand but it was too late. Alexis picked up the scent like a bloodhound.

"Is that Hunter? He's with you?"

"Yes. We just got in from a late dinner."

Not a lie, exactly. Not the whole truth, either. There were some things her boss simply didn't need to know.

"Good," Alexis was saying. "He can look over the JPEGs I just emailed you from the photo shoot at Cartier. I marked the one we're going to use with the blurb about your engagement."

"We'll take a look at them and get back to you."

"Tonight, kiddo. I want the story in this month's issue."

"Okay." Sighing, Sarah closed the flaps of her jacket and fastened the top button one-handed. "Shoot me the blurb, too."

"Don't worry about it. It's only a few lines."

The too-bland assurance set off an internal alarm.

"Send it, Alexis."

"All right, all right. But I want it back tonight, too."

She cut the connection, and Sarah sank back onto the cushions. Dev sat in his corner, one arm stretched across the sofa back. His shirttails hung open and his belt had somehow come unbuckled. He looked more than willing to pick up where they'd left off, but Sarah's common sense had kicked in. Or rather her sense of self-preservation.

"Saved by the bell," she said with an attempt at lightness. "At least now I won't have to improvise when Elise starts digging for details."

The phone pinged in her hand, signaling the arrival of a text message.

"That's the blurb Alexis wants to run with the pictures from Cartier. I'll pull it up with the photos so you can review them."

"No need." Dev pushed off the sofa, stuffed in his shirt and buckled his belt. "I trust you on this one."

"I'll make sure there are no naked body parts showing," she promised solemnly.

"You do that, and I'll make sure we're not interrupted next time."

"Next time?"

He dropped a quick kiss on her nose and grabbed his discarded suit coat.

"Oui, ma chérie," he said in his truly execrable French. "Next time."

Nine

Dev had a breakfast meeting with his people, who'd flown in the night before. That gave Sarah the morning to herself. A shame, really, because the day promised glorious sunshine and much warmer temperatures. Perfect for strolling the Left Bank with that special someone.

Which is what most of Paris seemed to be doing, she saw after coffee and a croissant at her favorite patisserie. The sight of so many couples, young, old and in between, rekindled some of the raw emotions Dev had generated last night.

In the bright light of day, Sarah couldn't believe she'd invited him to make love to her. Okay, she'd practically demanded it. Even now, as she meandered over the Pont de l'Archevêché, she felt her breasts tingle at the memory of his hands and mouth on them.

She stopped midway across the bridge. Pont de l'Archevêché translated to the Archbishop's Bridge in English, most likely because it formed a main means of transit for the clerics of Notre Dame. The cathedral's square towers rose on the right. Bookseller stalls and cafés crowded the broad avenue on the left. The Seine flowed dark and silky below. What intrigued her, though, were the padlocks of all shapes and sizes hooked through the bridge's waist-high, iron-mesh scrollwork. Some locks had tags attached, some were decorated with bright ribbons, some included small charms.

She'd noticed other bridges sporting locks, although none as heavily adorned as this one. They'd puzzled her but she hadn't really wondered about their significance. It became apparent a few moments after she spotted a pair of tourists purchasing a padlock from an enterprising lock seller at the far end of the bridge. The couple searched for an empty spot on the fancy grillwork to attach their purchase. Then they threw the key into the Seine and shared a long, passionate kiss.

When they walked off arm in arm, Sarah approached the lock seller. He was perched on an upturned wooden crate beside a pegboard displaying his wares. His hair sprouted like milky-white dandelion tufts from under his rusty-black beret. A cigarette hung from his lower lip.

"I've been away for a while," she said in her fluent Parisian. "When did this business with the locks begin?"

"Three years? Five? Who can remember?" His shoulders lifted in the quintessential Gallic shrug. "At first the locks appeared only at night, and they would be cut off each day. Now they are everywhere."

"So it seems."

Mistaking her for a native, he winked and shared his personal opinion of his enterprise. "The tourists, they eat this silly stuff up. As if they can lock in the feelings they have right now, today, and throw away the key. We French know better, yes?"

His cigarette bobbed. His gestures grew extravagant as he expounded his philosophy.

"To love is to take risks. To be free, not caged. To walk away if what you feel brings hurt to you or to your lover. Who would stay, or want to stay, where there is pain?"

The question was obviously rhetorical, so Sarah merely spread her hands and answered with a shrug.

She was still thinking about the encounter when she met Madame Girault for lunch later that day. She related the lock seller's philosophy to Elise, who belted out a raucous laugh that turned heads throughout the restaurant.

"My darling Sarah, I must beg to disagree!"

With her blond hair drawn into a tight bun that emphasized her high cheekbones and angular chin, Elise looked more like the Black Swan of her portrait. Her sly smile only heightened the resemblance.

"Locks and, yes, a little pain can add a delicious touch to an affair," she said, her eyes dancing. "And speaking of which…"

Her mouth took a sardonic tilt as a dark-haired man some twenty-five or thirty years her junior rose from his table and approached theirs.

"Ah, Elise, only one woman in all Paris has a laugh like yours. How are you, my love?"

"Very well. And you, Henri? Are you still dancing attendance on that rich widow I saw you with at the theater?"

"Sadly, she returned to Argentina before I extracted full payment for services rendered." His dark eyes drifted to Sarah. "But enough of such mundane matters. You must introduce me to your so-lovely companion."

"No, I must not. She's in Paris with her fiancé and has no need of your special skills." Elise flapped a hand and shooed him off. "Be a good boy and go away."

"If you insist…"

He gave a mocking half bow and returned to his table, only to sign the check and leave a few moments later. A fleeting look of regret crossed Elise's face as he wove his way toward the exit. Sighing, she fingered her glass.

"He was so inventive in bed, that one. So *very* inventive. But always in need of money. When I tired of emptying my purse for him, he threatened to sell pictures of me in certain, shall we say, exotic positions."

Sarah winced, but couldn't say anything. Any mention of the paparazzi and sensational photographs struck too close to home.

"Jean-Jacques sent men to convince him that would not be wise," Elise confided. "The poor boy was in a cast for weeks afterward."

The offhand comment doused the enjoyment Sarah had taken in Elise's company up to that point. Madame Girault's concept of love suddenly seemed more tawdry than amusing. Deliberately, Sarah changed the subject.

"I wonder how the negotiations are going? Dev said he thought they were close to a deal."

Clearly disinterested, Elise shrugged and snapped her fingers to summon their waiter.

Halfway across Paris, Dev had to force himself to focus on the columns of figures in the newly restructured agreement. It didn't help that his seat at the conference table offered a panoramic view of the pedestrians-only esplanade and iconic Grande Arche that dominated Paris's financial district. Workers by the hundreds were seated on the steps below the Grande Arche, their faces lifted to the sun while they enjoyed their lunch break.

One couple appeared to be enjoying more than the sun. Dev watched them share a touch, a laugh, a kiss. Abruptly, he pushed away from the table.

"Sorry," he said to the dozen or so startled faces that turned in his direction. "I need to make a call."

Jean-Jacques Girault scooted his chair away from the table, as well. "Let's all take a break. We'll reconvene in thirty minutes, yes? There'll be a catered lunch waiting when we return."

Dev barely waited for Girault to finish his little speech. The urge to talk to Sarah, to hear her voice, drove him through the maze of outer offices and into the elevator. A short while later he'd joined the throng on the steps below the Grande Arche.

It took him a moment to acknowledge the unfamiliar sensation that knifed through him as he dialed Sarah's number. It wasn't just the lust that had damned near choked him last night. It was that amorphous, indefinable feeling immortalized in so many sappy songs. Grimacing, he admitted the inescapable truth. He was in love, or close enough to it to make no difference.

Sarah answered on the second ring. "Hello, Dev. This must be mental telepathy. I was just talking about you."

"You were, huh?"

"How are the negotiations going?"

"They're going."

The sound of her voice did something stupid to his insides. To his head, too. With barely a second thought, he abandoned Girault and company to the team of sharks he'd flown in last night.

"We've been crunching numbers all morning. I'm thinking of letting my people handle the afternoon session. What do you have planned?"

"Nothing special."

"How about I meet you back at the hotel and we'll do nothing special together?"

He didn't intend to say what came next. Didn't have any control over the words. They just happened.

"Or maybe," he said, his voice going husky, "we can work on our next time."

A long silence followed his suggestion. When it stretched for several seconds, Dev kicked himself for his lack of finesse. Then she came back with a low, breathless response that damned near stopped his heart.

"I'll catch a cab and meet you at the hotel."

* * *

Sarah snapped her phone shut and sent Madame Girault a glance that was only a shade apologetic. "That was Dev. I'm sorry, but I have to go."

Elise looked startled for a moment. But only a moment. Then her face folded into envious lines.

"Go," she ordered with a wave of one hand. "Paris is the city of love, after all. And I think yours, *ma petite,* is one that deserves a lock on the Archbishop's Bridge."

Sarah wanted to believe that was what sent her rushing out of the restaurant. Despite the lock seller's philosophical musings, despite hearing the details of Elise's sordid little affair, she wanted desperately to believe that what she felt for Dev could stand the test of time.

That hope took a temporary hit when she caught up with the dark-haired, dark-eyed Henri on the pavement outside of the restaurant. He'd just hailed a cab, but generously offered it to her instead.

Or not so generously. His offer to escort her to her hotel and fill her afternoon hours with unparalleled delight left an unpleasant taste in Sarah's mouth. Unconsciously, she channeled Grandmama.

"I think not, monsieur."

The haughty reply sent him back a pace. The blank surprise on his face allowed Sarah more than enough time to slide into the cab and tell the driver her destination. Then she slammed the door and forgot Henri, forgot Elise, forgot everything but the instant hunger Dev's call had sparked in her.

She wrestled with that hunger all the way back to the hotel. Her cool, rational, practical-by-necessity self kept asserting that her arrangement with Dev Hunter was just that, an arrangement. A negotiated contract that would soon conclude. If she made love with him, as she desperately wanted to do, she'd simply be satisfying a short-term physical need while possibly setting herself up for long-term regrets.

The other side of her, the side she usually kept so sternly repressed, echoed Gina at her giddiest. Why not grab a little pleasure? Taste delight here, now, and let tomorrow take care of itself?

As was happening all too frequently with Dev, giddy and greedy vanquished cool and rational. By the time Sarah burst out of the elevator and headed down the hall toward her room, heat coursed through her, hot and urgent. The sight of Dev leaning against the wall beside the door to her room sent her body temperature soaring up another ten degrees.

"What took you so long?" he demanded.

Snatching the key card from her hand, he shoved it into the lock. Two seconds after the door opened, he had her against the entryway wall.

"I hope you had a good lunch. We won't be coming up for food or drink anytime soon."

The bruising kiss spiked every one of Sarah's senses. She tasted him, drank in his scent, felt his hips slam hers against the wall.

He kicked the door shut. Or did she? She didn't know, didn't care. Dev's hands were all over her at that point. Unbuttoning her blouse. Hiking up her skirt. Shoving down her bikini briefs.

Panting, greedy, wanting him so much she ached with it, she struggled out of her blouse. Kicked her shoes off and the panties free of her ankles. Hooked one leg around his thighs.

"Sarah." It was a groan and a plea. "Let's take this to the bedroom."

Mere moments later she was naked and stretched out on the king-size bed. Her avid gaze devoured Dev as he stood beside the bed and shed his clothing.

She'd seen portions of him last night. Enough to confirm that he ranked much higher than number three on her personal top ten list. Those glimpses didn't even begin to compare with the way he looked now with his black hair catching the afternoon light and his blue eyes fired with need. Every muscle in his long, lean body looked taut and eager. He was hard for her, and hungry, and so ready that Sarah almost yelped when he turned away.

"What are you doing?"

"Making sure you don't regret this."

Her dismay became a wave of relief when she saw him extract a condom from the wallet in his discarded pants. She wasn't on the pill. She'd stopped months ago. Or was it years? Sarah couldn't remember. She suspected her decision to quit birth control had a lot to do with the realization that taking care of Grandmama and keeping a roof over their heads were more important to her than casual sex.

Showed what she knew. There was nothing casual about this sex, however. The need for it, the gnawing hunger for it, consumed her.

No! Her mind screamed the denial even as she opened her arms to Dev. This wasn't just sex. This wasn't just raw need. This was so elemental. So…so French. Making love in the afternoon. With a man who filled her, physically, emotionally, every way that mattered.

His hips braced against hers. His knees pried hers apart. Eagerly, Sarah opened her legs and her arms and her heart to him. When he eased into her, she hooked her calves around his and rose up to meet his first, slow thrusts. Then the pace picked up. In. Out. In again.

Soon, *too* soon, dammit, her vaginal muscles began to quiver and her belly contracted. She tried to suppress the spasms. Tried to force her muscles to ease their greedy grip. She wanted to build to a steady peak, spin the pleasure as long as she could.

Her body refused to listen to her mind. The tight, spiraling sensation built to a wild crescendo. Panting, Sarah arched her neck. A moment later, she was flying, sailing, soaring. Dev surged into her, went taut and rode to the crest with her. Then he gave a strangled grunt and collapsed on top of her.

* * *

Sarah was still shuddering with the aftershocks when he whispered a French phrase into her ear. Her eyes flew open. Her jaw dropped.

"What did you say?"

He levered up on one elbow. A flush rode high in his cheeks and his blue eyes were still fever bright, but he managed a semicoherent reply.

"I was trying to tell you I adore you."

Sarah started giggling and couldn't stop. No easy feat with 180 plus pounds of naked male pinning her to the sheets.

A rueful grin sketched across Dev's face. "Okay, what did I really say?"

"It sounded…it sounded…" Helpless with laughter, she gasped for breath. "It sounded like you want to hang an ornament on me."

"Yeah, well, that, too." His grin widening, he leaned down and dropped a kiss on her left breast. "Here. And here…"

He grazed her right breast, eased down to her belly.

"And here, and…"

"Dev!"

Pleasure rippled in waves across the flat plane of her stomach. She wouldn't have believed she could become so aroused so fast. Particularly after that shattering orgasm. Dev, on the other hand, was lazy and loose and still flaccid.

"Don't you need to, uh, take a little time to recharge?"

"I do." His voice was muffled, his breath hot against her skin. "Doesn't mean you have to. Unless you want to?"

He raised his head and must have seen the answer in her face. Waggling his brows, he lowered his head again. Sarah gasped again when his tongue found her now supersensitized center.

The climax hit this time without warning. She'd just reached up to grip the headboard and bent a knee to avoid a cramp when everything seemed to shrink to a single, white-hot nova. The next second, the star exploded. Pleasure pulsed through her body. Groaning, she let it flow before it slowly, exquisitely ebbed.

When she opened her eyes again, Dev looked smug and pretty damn pleased with himself. With good reason, she thought, drifting on the last eddies. She sincerely hoped he still needed some time to recharge. She certainly did!

To her relief, he stretched out beside her and seemed content to just laze. She nestled her head on his arm and let her thoughts drift back to his mangled French. He said he'd been trying to tell her that he adored her. What did that mean, exactly?

She was trying to find a way to reintroduce the subject when the phone buzzed. His this time, not hers. With a muffled grunt, Dev reached across her and checked his phone's display.

"Sorry," he said with a grimace. "I told them not to call unless they were about to slam up against our own version of a fiscal cliff. I'd better take this."

"Go ahead. I'll hit the bathroom."

She scooped up the handiest article of clothing, which happened to be Dev's shirt, and padded into the bathroom. The tiles felt cool and smooth against her bare feet. The apparition that appeared in the gilt-edged mirrors made her gasp.

"Good grief!"

Her hair could have provided a home for an entire flock of sparrows. Whatever makeup she'd started out with this morning had long since disappeared. She was also sporting one whisker burn on her chin and another on her neck. Shuddering at the thought of what Elise Girault would say if she saw the telltale marks, Sarah ran the taps and splashed cold water on her face and throat.

That done, she eyed the bidet. So practical for Europeans, so awkward for most Americans. Practical won hands down in this instance. Clean and refreshed, Sarah reentered the bedroom just as Dev was zipping up his pants.

"Uh-oh. Looks like your negotiators ran into that cliff."

"Ran into it, hell. According to my chief of production, they soared right over the damned thing and are now in a free fall."

"That doesn't sound good."

Detouring to her closet, she exchanged Dev's shirt for the thigh-length, peony-decorated silk robe Gina had given her for her birthday last year.

"It's all part of the game," he said as she handed him back his shirt. "Girault's just a little better at it than I gave him credit for."

The comment tripped a reminder of Elise's disclosures at lunch. Sarah debated for a moment over whether she should share them with Dev, then decided he needed to know the kind of man he would be doing business with.

"Elise said something today about her husband that surprised me."

Dev looked up from buttoning his shirt. "What was that?"

"Supposedly, Jean-Jacques sent some goons to rough up one of her former lovers. The guy had threatened to sell pictures of her to the tabloids."

"Interesting. I would have thought Girault man enough to do the job himself. I certainly would have." He scooped up his tie and jacket and gave her a quick kiss. "I'll call as soon as I have a fix on when we'll break for dinner."

Sarah nodded, but his careless remark about going after Elise's lover for trying to sell pictures of her had struck home. The comment underscored his contempt for certain members of her profession. How much would it take, she wondered uneasily, for him to lump her in with the sleaziest among them?

Ten

Still troubled by Dev's parting comment, Sarah knotted the sash to her robe and stepped out onto her little balcony. She'd lost herself in the view before, but this time the seemingly endless vista of chimneys and gray slate roofs didn't hold as much interest as her bird's-eye view of the street four stories below.

The limo Dev had called for idled a few yards from the hotel's entrance. When he strode out of the hotel, the sight of him once again outfitted in his business attire gave Sarah's heart a crazy bump. She couldn't help contrasting that with the image of his sleek, naked body still vivid in her mind.

The uniformed driver jumped out to open the rear passenger door. Dev smiled and said a few words to him, inaudible from Sarah's height, and ducked to enter the car. At the last moment he paused and glanced up. When he spotted her, the friendly smile he'd given the driver warmed into something so private and so sensual that she responded without thinking.

Touching her fingers lightly to her lips, she blew him a kiss—and was immediately embarrassed by the gesture. It was so schmaltzy, and so out of character for her. More like something Gina might do. Yet she remained on the balcony like some lovelorn Juliet long after Dev had driven off.

Even worse, she couldn't summon the least desire to get dressed and meander through the streets. Peering into shop windows or people watching at a café didn't hold as much allure as it had before. She would rather wait until Dev finished with his meeting and they could meander together.

She'd take a long, bubbly bath instead, she decided. But first she had catch up on her email. And call Grandmama. And try Gina again. Maybe this time her sister would answer the damned phone.

Gina didn't, but Sarah caught the duchess before she went out for her morning constitutional. She tried to temper her habitual concern with a teasing note.

"You won't overdo it, will you?"

"My darling Sarah," Charlotte huffed. "If I could walk almost forty miles through a war-torn country with an infant in my arms, I can certainly stroll a few city blocks."

Wisely, Sarah refrained from pointing out that the duchess had made the first walk more than fifty years ago.

"Have you heard from Gina?" she asked instead.

"No, have you?"

"Not since she texted me that she was flitting off to Switzerland."

She'd tried to keep her the response casual, but the duchess knew her too well.

"Listen to me, Sarah Elizabeth Marie-Adele. Your sister may act rashly on occasion, but she's a St. Sebastian. Whatever you think she may be up to, she won't bring shame on her family or her name."

The urge to tell her grandmother about the missing medallion was so strong that Sarah had to bite her lip to keep from blurting it out. That would only lead to a discussion of how she'd become involved with Dev, and she wasn't

ready to explain that, either. Thankfully, her grandmother
was content to let the subject drop.

"Now tell me about Paris," she commanded. "Has Devon
taken you to Café Michaud yet?"

"Not yet, but he said you'd given him strict orders to do
so. Oh, and he had his people work minor miracles to get
us into the Hôtel Verneuil on such short notice."

"He did? How very interesting."

She sounded so thoughtful—and so much like a cat that
had just lapped up a bowl of cream—that Sarah became
instantly suspicious.

"What other instructions did you give him?"

"None."

"Come on. Fess up. What other surprises do I have in
store?"

A soft sigh came through the phone. "You're in Paris,
with a handsome, virile man. One whom I suspect is more
than capable of delivering surprises of his own."

Sarah gave a fervent prayer of thanks that the duchess
hadn't yet mastered the FaceTime app on her phone. If she
had, she would have seen her elder granddaughter's cheeks
flame at the thought of how much she'd *already* enjoyed
her handsome, virile fiancé.

"I'll talk to you tomorrow, Grandmama. Give Maria
my love."

She hung up, marveling again at how readily everyone
seemed to have accepted Dev Hunter's sudden appearance
in their lives. Grandmama. Maria. Alexis. Sarah herself.
Would they accept his abrupt departure as readily?

Would they have to?

Sarah was no fool. Nor was she blind. She could tell
Dev felt at least some of the same jumbled emotions she
did. Mixed in with the greedy hunger there was the shared
laughter, the seduction of this trip, the growing delight in
each other's company. Maybe, just maybe, there could be
love, too.

She refused to even speculate about anything beyond that. Their evolving relationship was too new, too fragile, to project vary far ahead. Still, she couldn't help humming the melody from Edith Piaf's classic, "La Vie En Rose," as she started for the bathroom and a long, hot soak.

The house phone caught her halfway there. She detoured to the desk and answered. The caller identified himself as Monsieur LeBon, the hotel's manager, and apologized profusely for disturbing her.

"You're not disturbing me, monsieur."

"Good, good." He hesitated, then seemed to be choosing his words carefully. "I saw Monsieur Hunter leave a few moments ago and thought perhaps I might catch you alone."

"Why? Is there a problem?"

"I'm not sure. Do you by chance know a gentleman by the name of Henri Lefèvre?"

"I don't recognize the name."

"Aha! I thought as much." LeBon gave a small sniff. "There was something in his manner…"

"What has this Monsieur Lefèvre to do with me?"

"He approached our receptionist earlier this afternoon and claimed you and he were introduced by a mutual acquaintance. He couldn't remember your name, however. Only that you were a tall, slender American who spoke excellent French. And that you mentioned you were staying at the Hôtel Verneuil."

The light dawned. It had to be Elise's former lover. He must have heard her give the cabdriver instructions to the hotel.

"The receptionist didn't tell him my name, did she?"

"You may rest assured she did not! Our staff is too well trained to disclose information on any of our guests. She referred the man to me, and I sent him on his way."

"Thank you, Monsieur LeBon. Please let me know immediately if anyone else inquires about me."

"Of course, Lady Sarah."

The call from the hotel manager dimmed a good bit of Sarah's enjoyment in her long, bubbly soak. She didn't particularly like the fact that Elise's smarmy ex-lover had tracked her to the hotel.

Dev called just moments after she emerged from the tub. Sounding totally disgusted, he told her he intended to lock everyone in the conference room until they reached a final agreement.

"The way it looks now that might be midnight or later. Sorry, Sarah. I won't be able to keep our dinner date."

"Don't worry about that."

"Yeah, well, I'd much rather be with you than these clowns. I'm about ready to tell Girault and company to shove it."

Sarah didn't comment. She couldn't, given the staggering sums involved in his negotiations. But she thought privately he was taking a risk doing business with someone who hired thugs to pound on his wife's lover.

Briefly, she considered telling Dev that same lover had shown up at the hotel this afternoon but decided against it. He had enough on his mind at the moment and Monsieur LeBon appeared to have taken care of the matter.

She spent what remained of the afternoon and most of the evening on her laptop, with only a short break for soup and a salad ordered from room service. She had plenty of work to keep her busy and was satisfied with the two layouts she'd mocked up when she finally quit. She'd go in to the offices on rue Balzac tomorrow to view the layouts on the twenty-five-inch monitor.

Unless Dev finished negotiations tonight as he swore he would do. Then maybe they'd spend the day together. And the night. And…

Her belly tightening at the possibilities, she curled up in bed with the ebook she'd downloaded. She got through only a few pages before she dozed off.

* * *

The phone jerked her from sleep. She fumbled among the covers, finally found it and came more fully awake when she recognized Dev's number.

"Did you let them all out of the conference room?" she asked with a smile.

"I did. They're printing the modified contracts as we speak. They'll be ready to sign tomorrow morning."

"Congratulations!"

She was happy for him, she really was, even if it meant the termination of their arrangement.

"I'm on my way back to the hotel. Is it too late for a celebration?"

"I don't know. What time is it?"

"Almost one."

"No problem. Just give me a few minutes to get dressed. Do you have someplace special in mind? If not, I know several great cafés that stay open until 2:00 a.m."

"Actually, I was hoping for a private celebration. No dressing required."

She could hear the smile in his voice, and something more. Something that brought Gina forcefully to mind. Her sister always claimed she felt as though she was tumbling through time and space whenever she fell in love. Sarah hadn't scoffed but she *had* chalked the hyperbole up to another Gina-ism.

How wrong she was. And how right Gina was. That was exactly how Sarah felt now. As though Dev had kicked her feet out from under her and she was on some wild, uncontrollable slide.

"A private celebration sounds good to me," she got out breathlessly.

She didn't change out of the teddy and bikini briefs she'd worn to bed, but she did throw on the peony robe and make a dash to the bathroom before she answered Dev's knock.

As charged up as he'd sounded on the phone, she half expected him to kick the door shut and pin her against the wall again. Okay, she kind of hoped he would.

He didn't, but Sarah certainly couldn't complain about his altered approach. The energy was there, and the exultation from having closed his big deal. Yet the hands that cupped her face were incredibly gentle, and the kiss he brushed across her mouth was so tender she almost melted from the inside out.

"Jean-Jacques told me to thank you," he murmured against her lips.

"For what?"

"He thinks I finally agreed to his company's design for the pneumatic turbine assembly because I was so damned anxious to get back to you."

"Oh, no!"

She pulled back in dismay. She had no idea what a pneumatic turbine assembly was, but it sounded important.

"You didn't concede anything critical, did you?"

"Nah. I always intended to accept their design. I just used it as my ace in the hole to close the deal. *And* to get back to you."

He bent and brushed her mouth again. When he raised his head, the look in his eyes started Sarah on another wild spin through time and space.

"I don't want to risk any more mangled verbs," he said with a slow smile, "so I'll stick to English this time. I love you, Sarah St. Sebastian."

"Since...? Since when?"

He appeared to give the matter some consideration. "Hard to say. I have to admit it started with a severe case of lust."

She would have to admit the same thing. Later. Right now she could only try to keep breathing as he raised her hand and angled it so the emerald caught the light.

"By the time I put this on your finger, though, I was

already strategizing ways to keep it there. I know I black-mailed you into this fake engagement, Sarah, but if I ask very politely and promise to be nice to your ditz of a sister, would you consider making it real?"

Although it went against a lifetime of ingrained habit, she didn't fire up in Gina's defense. Instead she drew her brows together.

"I need a minute to think about it."

Surprise and amusement and just a touch of uncertainty colored Dev's reply. "Take all the time you need."

She pursed her lips and gave the matter three or four seconds of fierce concentration.

"Okay."

"Okay you'll consider it, or okay you'll make it real?"

Laughing, Sarah hooked her arms around his neck. "I'm going with option B."

Dev hadn't made a habit of going on the prowl like so many crew dogs he'd flown with, but he'd racked up more than a few quality hours with women in half a dozen countries. Not until *this* woman, however, did he really appreciate the difference between having sex and making love. It wasn't her smooth, sleek curves or soft flesh or breathless little pants. It was the sum of all parts, the whole of her, the elegance that was Sarah.

And the fact that she was his.

He'd intended to make this loving slow and sweet, a sort of unspoken acknowledgment of the months and years of nights like this they had ahead. She blew those plans out of the water mere moments after Dev positioned her under him. Her body welcomed him, her heat fired his. The primitive need to possess her completely soon had him pinning her wrists to the sheets, his thrusts hard and deep. Her head went back. Her belly quivered. A moan rose from deep in her throat, and Dev took everything she had to give.

* * *

She was still half-asleep when he leaned over her early the next morning. "I've got to shower and change and get with Girault to sign the contracts. How about we meet for lunch at your grandmother's favorite café?"

"Mmm."

"Tell me the name of it again."

"Café Michaud," she muttered sleepily, "rue de Monttessuy."

"Got it. Café Michaud. Rue de Monttessuy. Twelve noon?"

"Mmm."

He took his time in the shower, answered several dozen emails, reviewed a bid solicitation on a new government contract and still made the ten o'clock signing session at Girault's office with time to spare.

The French industrialist was in a jovial mood, convinced he'd won a grudging, last-minute concession. Dev didn't disabuse him. After initialing sixteen pages and signing three, the two chief executives posed for pictures while their respective staffs breathed sighs of relief that the months of intense negotiations were finally done.

"How long do you remain in Paris?" Girault asked after pictures and another round of handshakes.

"I had planned to fly home as soon as we closed this deal, but I think now I'll take some downtime and stay over a few more days."

"A very wise decision," Girault said with a wink. "Paris is a different city entirely when explored with one you love. Especially when that one is as delightful as your Sarah."

"I won't argue with that. And speaking of my Sarah, we're meeting for lunch. I'll say goodbye now, Jean-Jacques."

"But no! Not goodbye. You must have dinner with Elise and me again before you leave. Now that we are partners, yes?"

"I'll see what Sarah has planned and get back to you."

* * *

The rue de Monttessuy was in the heart of Paris's 7th arrondissement. Tall, stately buildings topped with slate roofs crowded the sidewalks and offered a glimpse of the Eiffel Tower spearing into the sky at the far end of the street. Café Michaud sat midway down a long block, a beacon of color with its bright red awnings and window boxes filled with geraniums.

Since he was almost a half hour early, Dev had his driver drop him off at the intersection. He needed to stretch his legs, and he preferred to walk the half block rather than wait for Sarah at one of the café's outside tables. Maybe he could find something for her in one of the shops lining the narrow, cobbled street. Unlike the high-end boutiques and jeweler's showrooms on some of the more fashionable boulevards, these were smaller but no less intriguing.

He strolled past a tiny grocery with fresh produce displayed in wooden crates on either side of the front door, a chocolatier, a wine shop and several antique shops. One in particular caught his attention. Its display of military and aviation memorabilia drew him into the dim, musty interior.

His eyes went instantly to an original lithograph depicting Charles Lindbergh's 1927 landing at a Paris airfield after his historic solo transatlantic flight. The photographer had captured the shadowy images of the hundreds of Model As and Ts lined up at the airfield, their headlamps illuminating the grassy strip as the *Spirit of St. Louis* swooped out of the darkness.

"I'll take that," he told the shopkeeper.

The man's brows soared with surprise and just a touch of disdain for this naive American who made no attempt to bargain. Dev didn't care. He would have paid twice the price. He'd never thought of himself as particularly sentimental, but the key elements in the print—aviation and Paris—were what had brought him and Sarah together.

As if to compensate for his customer's foolishness, the shopkeeper threw in at no cost the thick cardboard tube the print had been rolled in when he himself had discovered it at a flea market.

Tube in hand, Dev exited the shop and started for the café. His pulse kicked when he spotted Sarah approaching from the opposite direction. She was on the other side of the street, some distance from the café, but he recognized her graceful walk and the silky brown hair topped by a jaunty red beret.

He picked up his pace, intending to cross at the next corner, when a figure half-hidden amid a grocer's produce display brought him to a dead stop. The man had stringy brown hair that straggled over the shoulders and a camera propped on the top crate. Its monster zoom lens was aimed directly at Sarah. While Dev stood there, his jaw torquing, the greaseball clicked off a half-dozen shots.

"What the hell are you doing?"

The photographer whipped around. He said something in French, but it was the careless shrug that fanned Dev's anger into fury.

"Bloodsucking parasites," he ground out.

The hand gripping the cardboard tube went white at the knuckles. His other hand bunched into a fist. Screw the lawsuits. He'd flatten the guy. The photographer read his intent and jumped back, knocking over several crates of produce in the process.

"Non, non!" He stumbled back, his face white with alarm under the greasy hair. "You don't…you don't understand, Monsieur Hunter. I am François. With *Beguile*. I shoot the photos for the story."

For the second time in as many moments, Dev froze. "The story?"

"Oui. We get the instructions from New York."

He thrust out the camera and angled the digital display.

His thumb beat a rapid tattoo as he clicked through picture after picture.

"But look! Here are you and Sarah having coffee. And here you walk along the Seine. And here she blows you a kiss from the balcony of her hotel room."

Pride overrode the photographer's alarm. A few clicks of the zoom button enlarged the shot on the screen.

"Do you see how perfectly she is framed? And the expression on her face after you drive away. Like one lost in a dream, yes? She stays like that long enough for me to shoot from three different angles."

The anger still hot in Dev's gut chilled. Ice formed in his veins.

"She posed for you?" he asked softly, dangerously.

The photographer glanced up, nervous again. He stuttered something about New York, but Dev wasn't listening. His gaze was locked on Sarah as she approached the café.

She'd posed for this guy. After making all those noises about allowing only that one photo shoot at Cartier, she'd caved to her boss's demands. He might have forgiven that. He had a harder time with the fact that she'd set this all up without telling him.

Dev left the photographer amid the produce. Jaw tight, he stalked toward the café. Sarah was still a block away on the other side of the street. He was about to cross when a white delivery van slowed to a rolling stop and blocked her from view. A few seconds later, Dev heard the thud of its rear doors slam. When the van cut a sharp left and turned down a narrow side street, the sidewalk Sarah had been walking along was empty.

Eleven

Dev broke into a run even before he fully processed what had just happened. All he knew for sure was that Sarah had been strolling toward him one moment and was gone the next. His brain scrambled for a rational explanation of her sudden disappearance. She could have ducked into a shop. Could have stopped to check something in a store window. His gut went with the delivery van.

Dev hit the corner in a full-out sprint and charged down the side street. He dodged a woman pushing a baby carriage, earned a curse from two men he almost bowled over. He could see the van up ahead, see its taillights flashing red as it braked for a stop sign.

He was within twenty yards when the red lights blinked off. Less than ten yards away when the van began another turn. The front window was halfway down. Through it Dev could see the driver, his gaze intent on the pedestrians streaming across the intersection and his thin black cigarillo sending spirals of smoke through the half-open window.

Dev calculated the odds on the fly. Go for the double rear doors or aim for the driver? He risked losing the van if

the rear doors were locked and the vehicle picked up speed
after completing the turn. He also risked causing an accident if he jumped into traffic in the middle of a busy intersection and planted himself in front of the van.

He couldn't take that chance on losing it. With a desperate burst of speed, he cut the corner and ran into the
street right ahead of an oncoming taxi. Brakes squealing,
horn blaring, the cab fishtailed. Dev slapped a hand on
its hood, pushed off and landed in a few yards ahead of
the now-rolling van. He put up both hands and shouted a
fierce command.

"Stop!"

He got a glimpse, just a glimpse, of the driver's face
through the windshield. Surprise, fear, desperation all
flashed across it in the half second before he hit the gas.

Well, hell! The son of a bitch was gunning straight for
him.

Dev jumped out of the way at the last second and leaped
for the van's door as the vehicle tried to zoom past. The
door was unlocked, thank God, although he'd been prepared to hook an arm inside the open window and pop the
lock if necessary. Wrenching the panel open, he got a bull-
dog grip on the driver's leather jacket.

"Pull over, dammit."

The man jerked the wheel, cursing and shouting and
trying frantically to dislodge him. The van swerved. More
horns blasted.

"Dev!"

The shout came from the back of the van. From Sarah.
He didn't wait to hear more. His fist locked on the driver's leather jacket, he put all his muscle into a swift yank.
The bastard's face slammed into the steering wheel. Bone
crunched. Blood fountained. The driver slumped.

Reaching past him, Dev tore the keys from the ignition.
The engine died, but the van continued to roll toward a car
that swerved wildly but couldn't avoid a collision. Metal

crunched metal as both vehicles came to an abrupt stop, and Dev fumbled for the release for the driver's seat belt. He dragged the unconscious man out and let him drop to the pavement. Scrambling into the front seat, he had one leg over the console to climb into the rear compartment when the back doors flew open and someone jumped out.

It wasn't Sarah. She was on her knees in the back. A livid red welt marred one cheek. A roll of silver electrical tape dangled from a wide strip wrapped around one wrist. Climbing over the console, Dev stooped beside her.

"Are you okay?"

"Yes."

Her eyes were wide and frightened, but the distant wail of a siren eased some of their panic. Dev tore his glance from her to the open rear doors and the man running like hell back down the side street.

"Stay here and wait for the police. I'm going after that bastard."

"Wait!" She grabbed his arm. "You don't need to chase him! I know who he is."

He swung back. "You *know* him?"

When she nodded, suspicion knifed into him like a serrated blade. His fists bunched, and a distant corner of his mind registered the fact that he'd lost the lithograph sometime during the chase. The rest of him staggered under a sudden realization.

"This is part of it, isn't it? This big abduction scene?"

"Scene?"

She sounded so surprised he almost believed her. Worse, dammit, he wanted to believe her!

"It's okay," he ground out. "You can drop the act. I bumped into the photographer from *Beguile* back there on rue de Monttessuy. We had quite a conversation."

Her color drained, making the red welt across her cheek look almost obscene by contrast. "You...you talked to a photographer from my magazine?"

"Yeah, Lady Sarah, I did. François told me about the shoot. Showed me some of the pictures he's already taken. I'll have to ask him to send me the one of you on the balcony. You make a helluva Juliet."

The sirens were louder now. Their harsh, up-and-down bleat almost drowned out her whisper.

"And you think we…me, this photographer, my magazine…you think we staged an abduction?"

"I'm a little slow. It took me a while to understand the angle. I'm betting your barracuda of a boss dreamed it up. Big, brave Number Three rescues his beautiful fiancée from would-be kidnappers."

She looked away, and her silence cut even deeper than Dev's suspicion. He'd hoped she would go all huffy, deny at least some of her part in this farce. Apparently, she couldn't.

Well, Sarah and her magazine could damned well live with the consequences of their idiotic scheme. At the least, they were looking at thousands of dollars in vehicle damage. At the worst, reconstructive surgery for the driver whose face Dev had rearranged.

Thoroughly disgusted, he took Sarah's arm to help her out of the van. She shook off his hold without a word, climbed down and walked toward the squad car now screeching to a halt. Two officers exited. One went to kneel beside the moaning van driver. The other soon centered on Sarah as the other major participant in the incident. She communicated with him in swift, idiomatic French. He took notes the entire time, shooting the occasional glance at Dev that said his turn would come.

It did, but not until an ambulance had screamed up and two EMTs went to work on the driver. At the insistence of the officer who'd interviewed Sarah, a third medical tech examined her. The tech was shining a penlight into her pupils when the police officer turned his attention to Dev. Switching to English, he took down Dev's name, address

while in Paris and cell-phone number before asking for his
account of the incident.

He'd had time to think about it. Rather than lay out his
suspicion that the whole thing was a publicity stunt, he
stuck to the bare facts. He'd spotted Sarah walking toward
him. Saw the van pull up. Saw she was gone. Gave chase.

The police officer made more notes, then flipped back a
few pages. "So, Monsieur Hunter, are you also acquainted
with Henri Lefèvre?"

"Who?"

"The man your fiancée says snatched her off the street
and threw her into the back of this van."

"No, I'm not acquainted with him."

"But you know Monsieur Girault and his wife?"

Dev's eyes narrowed as he remembered Sarah telling
him about the goons Girault had employed to do his dirty
work. Was Lefèvre one of those goons? Was Jean-Jacques
somehow mixed up in all this?

"Yes," he replied, frowning, "I know Monsieur Girault
and his wife. How are they involved in this incident?"

"Mademoiselle St. Sebastian says Lefèvre is Madame
Girault's former lover. He came to their table while they
were at lunch yesterday. She claims Madame Girault identified him as a gigolo, one who tried to extort a large sum
of money from her. We'll verify that with madame herself, of course."

Dev's stomach took a slow dive. Christ! Had he mis-
read the situation? The kidnapping portion of it, anyway?

"Your fiancée also says that the manager of your hotel
told her Lefèvre made inquiries as to her identity." The officer glanced up from his notes. "Are you aware of these
inquiries, Monsieur Hunter?"

"No."

The police officer's expression remained carefully neutral, but he had to be thinking the same thing Dev was.

What kind of a man didn't know a second- or third-class gigolo was sniffing after his woman?

"Do you have any additional information you can provide at this time, Monsieur Hunter?"

"No."

"Very well. Mademoiselle St. Sebastian insists she sustained no serious injury. If the EMTs agree, I will release her to return to your hotel. I must ask you both not to leave Paris, however, until you have spoken with detectives from our *Brigade criminelle*. They will be in touch with you."

Dev and Sarah took a taxi back to the hotel. She stared out the window in stony silence while he searched for a way to reconcile his confrontation with the photographer and his apparently faulty assumption about the attempted kidnapping. He finally decided on a simple apology.

"I'm sorry, Sarah. I jumped too fast to the wrong conclusion."

She turned her head. Her distant expression matched her coolly polite tone. "No need to apologize. I can understand how you reached that conclusion."

Dev reached for her hand, trying to bridge the gap. She slid it away and continued in the same, distant tone.

"Just for the record, I didn't know the magazine had put a photographer on us."

"I believe you."

It was too little, too late. He realized that when she shrugged his comment aside.

"I am aware, however, that Alexis wanted to exploit the story, so I take full responsibility for this invasion of your privacy."

"*Our* privacy, Sarah."

"Your privacy," she countered quietly. "There is no us. It was all just a facade, wasn't it?"

"That's not what you said last night," Dev reminded her, starting to get a little pissed.

How the hell did he end up as the bad guy here? Okay, he'd blackmailed Sarah into posing as his fiancée. And, yes, he'd done his damnedest to finesse her into bed. Now that he had her there, though, he wanted more. Much more!

So did she. She'd admitted that last night. Dev wasn't about to let her just toss what they had together out the window.

"What happened to option B?" he pressed. "Making it real?"

She looked at him for a long moment before turning her face to the window again. "I have a headache starting. I'd rather not talk anymore, if you don't mind."

He minded. Big time. But the angry bruise rising on her cheek shut him up until they were back at the hotel.

"We didn't have lunch," he said in an effort to reestablish a common ground. "Do you want to try the restaurant here or order something from room service?"

"I'm not hungry." Still so cool, still so distant. "I'm going to lie down."

"You need ice to keep the swelling down on your cheek. I'll bring some to your room after I talk to Monsieur LeBon."

"There's ice in the minifridge in my room."

She left him standing in the lobby. Frustrated and angry and not sure precisely where he should target his ire, he stalked to the reception desk and asked to speak to the manager.

Sarah's first act when she reached her room was to call *Beguile*'s Paris offices. Although she didn't doubt Dev's account, she couldn't help hoping the photographer he'd spoken to was a freelancer or worked for some other publication. In her heart of hearts, she didn't want to believe *her* magazine had, in fact, assigned François to shoot pictures of her and Dev. Paul Vincent, the senior editor, provided the corroboration reluctantly.

"Alexis insisted, Sarah."

"I see."

She disconnected and stared blankly at the wall for several moments. How naive of her to trust Alexis to hold to her word. How stupid to feel so hurt that Dev would jump to the conclusion he had. Her throat tight, she tapped out a text message. It was brief and to the point.

I quit, effective immediately.

Then she filled the ice bucket, wrapped some cubes in a hand towel and shed her clothes. Crawling into bed, she put the ice on her aching cheek and pulled the covers over her head.

The jangle of the house phone dragged her from a stew of weariness and misery some hours later.

"I'm sorry to disturb you, Lady Sarah."

Grimacing, she edged away from the wet spot on the pillow left by the soggy hand towel. "What is it, Monsieur LeBon?"

"You have a call from *Brigade criminelle*. Shall we put it through?"

"Yes."

The caller identified herself as Marie-Renee Delacroix, an inspector in the division charged with investigating homicides, kidnappings, bomb attacks and incidents involving personalities. Sarah wanted to ask what category this investigation fell into but refrained. Instead she agreed to an appointment at police headquarters the next morning at nine.

"I've already spoken to Monsieur Hunter," the inspector said. "He'll accompany you."

"Fine."

"Just so you know, Mademoiselle St. Sebastian, this

meeting is a mere formality, simply to review and sign the official copy of your statement."

"That's all you need from me?"

"It is. We already had the van driver in custody, and we arrested Henri Lefèvre an hour ago. They've both confessed to attempting to kidnap you and hold you for ransom. Not that they could deny it," the inspector added drily. "Their fingerprints were all over the van, and no fewer than five witnesses saw Lefèvre jump out of it after the crash. We've also uncovered evidence that he's more than fifty thousand Euros in debt, much of which we believe he owes to a drug dealer not known for his patience."

A shudder rippled down Sarah's spine. She couldn't believe how close she'd come to being dragged into such a dark, ugly morass.

"Am I free to return to the United States after I sign my statement?"

"I'll have to check with the prosecutor's office, but I see no reason for them to impede your return given that Lefèvre and his accomplice have confessed. I'll confirm that when you come in tomorrow, yes?"

"Thank you."

She hung up and was contemplating going back to bed when there was a knock on her door.

"It's Dev, Sarah."

She wanted to take the coward's way out and tell him she didn't feel up to company, but she couldn't keep putting him off.

"Just a minute," she called through the door.

She detoured into the bedroom and threw on the clothes she'd dropped to the floor earlier. She couldn't do much about the bruise on her cheek, but she did rake a hand through her hair. Still, she felt messy and off center when she opened the door.

Dev had abandoned his suit coat but still wore the pleated pants and pale yellow dress shirt he'd had on earlier. The shirt was open at the neck, the cuffs rolled up. Sarah had to drag her reluctant gaze up to meet the deep blue of his eyes. They were locked on her cheek.

"Did you ice that?"

"Yes, I did. Come in."

He followed her into the sitting room. Neither of them sat. She gravitated to the window. He shoved his hands into his pants pockets and stood beside the sofa.

"Have you heard from Inspector Delacroix?"

"She just called. I understand we have an appointment with her at nine tomorrow morning."

"Did she tell you they've already obtained confessions?"

Sarah nodded and forced a small smile. "She also told me I could fly home after I signed the official statement. I was just about to call and make a reservation when you knocked."

"Without talking to me first?"

"I think we've said everything we needed to."

"I don't agree."

She scrubbed a hand down the side of her face. Her cheek ached. Her heart hurt worse. "Please, Dev. I don't want to beat this into the ground."

Poor verb choice, she realized when he ignored her and crossed the room to cup her chin. The ice hadn't helped much, Sarah knew. The bruise had progressed from red to a nasty purple and green.

"Did Lefèvre do this to you?"

The underlying savagery in the question had her pulling hastily away from his touch.

"No, he didn't. I hit something when he pushed me into the van."

The savagery didn't abate. If anything, it flared hotter and fiercer. "Good thing the bastard's in police custody."

Sarah struggled to get the discussion back on track. "Lefèvre doesn't matter, Dev."

"The hell he doesn't."

"Listen to me. What matters is that I didn't know Alexis had sicced a photographer on us. But even if she hadn't, some other magazine or tabloid would have picked up the story sooner or later. I'm afraid that kind of public scrutiny is something you and whoever you *do* finally get engaged to will have to live with."

"I'm engaged to you, Sarah."

"Not any longer."

Shoving her misery aside, she slid the emerald off her finger and held it out. He refused to take it.

"It's yours," he said curtly. "Part of your heritage. Whatever happens from here on out between us, you keep the Russian Rose."

The tight-jawed response only added to her aching unhappiness. "Our arrangement lasted only until you and Girault signed your precious contracts. That's done now. So are we."

She hadn't intended to sound so bitter. Dev had held to his end of their bargain. Every part of it. She was the one who'd almost defaulted. If not personally, then by proxy through Alexis.

But would Dev continue to hold to his end? The sudden worry that he might take his anger out on Gina pushed her into a rash demand for an assurance.

"I've fulfilled the conditions of our agreement, right? You won't go after my sister?"

She'd forgotten how daunting he could look when his eyes went hard and ice blue.

"No, Lady Sarah, I won't. And I think we'd better table this discussion until we've had more time to think things through."

"I've thought them through," she said desperately. "I'm going home tomorrow, Dev."

He leaned in, all the more intimidating because he didn't touch her, didn't raise his voice, didn't so much as blink.

"Think again, sweetheart."

Twelve

Left alone in her misery, Sarah opened her hand and stared at the emerald-and-gold ring. No matter what Dev said, she couldn't keep it.

Nor could she just leave it lying around. She toyed briefly with the thought of taking it downstairs and asking Monsieur LeBon to secure it in the hotel safe, but didn't feel up to explaining either her bruised cheek or the call from *Brigade criminelle*.

With an aching sense of regret for what might have been, she slipped the ring back on her finger. It would have to stay there until she returned it to Dev.

She was trying to make herself go into the bedroom and pack when a loud rumble from the vicinity of her middle reminded her she hadn't eaten since her breakfast croissant and coffee. She considered room service but decided she needed to get out of her room and clear her head. She also needed, as Dev had grimly instructed, to think more.

After a fierce internal debate, she picked up the house phone. A lifetime of etiquette hammered in by the duchess demanded she advise Dev of her intention to grab a bite at a local café. Fiancé or not, furious or not, he deserved the courtesy of a call.

Relief rolled through her in waves when he didn't answer. She left a quick message, then took the elevator to the lobby. Slipping out one of the hotel's side exits, she hiked up the collar of her sweater coat. It wasn't dusk yet, but the temperature was skidding rapidly from cool to cold.

As expected this time of day, the sidewalks and streets were crowded. Parisians returning from work made last-minute stops at grocers and patisseries. Taxis wove their erratic path through cars and bicycles. Sarah barely noticed the throng. Her last meeting with Dev still filled her mind. Their tense confrontation had shaken her almost as much as being snatched off the street and tossed into a delivery van like a sack of potatoes.

He had every right to be angry about the photographer, she conceded. She was furious, too. What had hurt most, though, was Dev's assumption that *Beguile* had staged the kidnapping. And that Sarah was part of the deception. How could he love her, yet believe she would participate in a scam like that?

The short answer? He couldn't.

As much as she wanted to, Sarah couldn't escape that brutal truth. She'd let Paris seduce her into thinking she and Dev shared something special. Come so close to believing that what they felt for each other would merit a padlock on the Archbishop's Bridge. Aching all over again for what might have been, she ducked into the first café she encountered.

A waiter with three rings piercing his left earlobe and a white napkin folded over his right forearm met her at the door. His gaze flickered to the ugly bruise on her cheek and away again.

"Good evening, madame."

"Good evening. A table for one, please."

Once settled at a table in a back corner, she ordered

without glancing at the menu. A glass of red table wine and a croque-monsieur—the classic French version of a grilled ham and cheese topped with béchamel sauce—was all she wanted. All she could handle right now. That became apparent after the first few sips of wine.

Her sandwich arrived in a remarkably short time given this was Paris, where even the humblest café aimed for gastronomic excellence. Accompanied by a small salad and thin, crisp fries, it should have satisfied her hunger. Unfortunately, she never got to enjoy it. She took a few forkfuls of salad and nibbled a fry, but just when she was about to bite into her sandwich she heard her name.

"Lady Sarah, granddaughter to Charlotte St. Sebastian, grand duchess of the tiny duchy once known as Karlenburgh."

Startled, she glanced up at the flat screen TV above the café's bar. While Sarah sat frozen with the sandwich halfway to her mouth, one of a team of two newscasters gestured to an image that came up on the display beside her. It was a photo of her and Gina and Grandmama, one of the rare publicity shots the duchess had allowed. It'd been taken at a charity event a number of years ago, before the duchess had sold her famous pearls. The perfectly matched strands circled her neck multiple times before draping almost to her waist.

"The victim of an apparent kidnapping attempt," the announcer intoned, "Lady Sarah escaped injury this afternoon during a dramatic rescue by her fiancé, American industrialist Devon Hunter."

Dread churned in the pit of Sarah's stomach as the still image gave way to what looked like an amateur video captured on someone's phone camera. It showed traffic swerving wildly as Dev charged across two lanes and planted himself in front of oncoming traffic.

Good God! The white van! It wasn't going to stop!

Her heart shot into her throat. Unable to breathe, she saw

Dev dodge aside at the last moment, then leap for the van door. When he smashed the driver's face into the wheel, Sarah gasped. Blobs of béchamel sauce oozed from the sandwich hanging from her fork and plopped unnoticed onto her plate. She'd been in the back of the van. She hadn't known how Dev had stopped it, only that he had.

Stunned by his reckless courage, she watched as the street scene gave way to another video. This one was shot on the steps of the Palais de Justice. Henri Lefèvre was being led down the steps to a waiting police transport. Uniformed officers gripped his arms. Steel cuffs shackled his wrists. A crowd of reporters waited at the bottom of the steps, shouting questions that Lefèvre refused to answer.

When the news shifted to another story, Sarah lowered her now-mangled sandwich. Her mind whirled as she tried to sort through her chaotic thoughts. One arrowed through all the others. She knew she had to call her grandmother. Now. Before the story got picked up by the news at home, if it hadn't already. Furious with herself for not thinking of that possibility sooner, she hit speed dial.

To her infinite relief, the duchess had heard nothing about the incident. Sarah tried to downplay it by making the kidnappers sound like bungling amateurs. Charlotte was neither amused nor fooled.

"Were you the target," she asked sharply, "or Devon?"

"Devon, of course. Or rather his billions."

"Are you sure? There may still be some fanatics left in the old country. Not many after all this time, I would guess. But your grandfather… Those murderous death squads…" Her voice fluttered. "They hated everything our family stood for."

"These men wanted money," Sarah said gently, "and Dev made them extremely sorry they went after it the way they did. One of them is going to need a whole new face."

"Good!"

The duchess had regained her bite, and her granddaughter breathed a sigh of relief. Too soon, it turned out.

"Bring Devon home with you, Sarah. I want to thank him personally. And tell him I see no need for a long engagement," Charlotte added briskly. "Too many brides today spend months, even years, planning their weddings. I thank God neither of my granddaughters are prone to such dithering."

"Grandmama…"

"Gina tends to leap before she looks. You, my darling, are more cautious. More deliberate. But when you choose, you choose wisely. In this instance, I believe you made an excellent choice."

Sarah couldn't confess that she hadn't precisely chosen Dev. Nor was she up to explaining that their relationship was based on a lie. All she could do was try to rein in the duchess.

"I'm not to the point of even thinking about wedding plans, Grandmama. I just got engaged."

And unengaged, although Dev appeared to have a different take on the matter.

"You don't have to concern yourself with the details, dearest. I'll call the Plaza and have Andrew take care of everything."

"Good grief!" Momentarily distracted, Sarah gasped. "Is Andrew still at the Plaza?"

Her exclamation earned an icy retort. "The younger generation may choose to consign seniors to the dustbin," the duchess returned frigidly. "Some of us are not quite ready to be swept out with the garbage."

Uh-oh. Before Sarah could apologize for the unintended slight, Charlotte abandoned her lofty perch and got down to business.

"How about the first weekend in May? That's such a lovely month for a wedding."

"Grandmama! It's mid-April now!"

"Didn't you hear me a moment ago? Long engagements are a bore."

"But…but…" Scrambling, Sarah grabbed at the most likely out. "I'm sure the Plaza is booked every weekend in May for the next three years."

Her grandmother heaved a long-suffering sigh. "Sarah, dearest, did I never tell you about the reception I hosted for the Sultan of Oman?"

"I don't think so."

"It was in July…no, August of 1962. Quite magnificent, if I do say so myself. President Kennedy and his wife attended, of course, as did the Rockefellers. Andrew was a very new, very junior waiter at the time. But the letter I sent to his supervisor commending his handling of an embarrassingly inebriated presidential aide helped catapult him to his present exalted position."

How could Sarah possibly respond to that? Swept along on a relentless tidal wave, she gripped the phone as the duchess issued final instructions. "Talk to Devon, dearest. Make sure the first weekend in May is satisfactory for him. And tell him I'll take care of everything."

Feeling almost as dazed as she had when Elise Girault's smarmy ex-lover manhandled her into that white van, Sarah said goodbye. Her meal forgotten, she sat with her phone in hand for long moments. The call to her grandmother had left her more confused, more torn.

Dev had risked his life for her. And that was after he'd confronted the photographer from *Beguile*. As angry as he'd been about her magazine stalking him, he'd still raced to her rescue. Then, of course, he'd accused her of being party to the ruse. As much as she wanted to, Sarah couldn't quite get past the disgust she'd seen in his face at that moment.

Yet he'd also shown her moments of incredible tenderness in their short time together. Moments of thoughtfulness and laughter and incredible passion. She couldn't get past those, either.

Or the fact that she'd responded to him so eagerly. So damned joyously. However they'd met, whatever odd circumstances had thrown them together, Dev Hunter stirred—and satisfied—a deep, almost primal feminine hunger she'd never experienced before.

The problem, Sarah mused as she paid her check and walked out into the deepening dusk, was that everything had happened so quickly. Dev's surprise appearance at her office. His bold-faced offer of a deal. Their fake engagement. This trip to Paris. She'd been caught up in the whirlwind since the day Dev had showed up at her office and tilted her world off its axis. The speed of it, the intensity of it, had magnified emotions and minimized any chance to catch her breath.

What they needed, she decided as she keyed the door to her room, was time and some distance from each other. A cooling-off period, after which they could start over. Assuming Dev wanted to start over, of course. Bracing herself for what she suspected would be an uncomfortable discussion, she picked up the house phone and called his room.

He answered on the second ring. "Hunter."

"It's Sarah."

"I got your message. Did you have a good dinner?"

She couldn't miss the steel under the too-polite query. He wasn't happy that she'd gone to eat without him.

"I did, thank you. Can you come down to my room? Or I'll come to yours, if that's more convenient."

"More convenient for what?"

All right. She understood he was still angry. As Grandmama would say, however, that was no excuse for boorishness.

"We need to finish the conversation we started earlier," she said coolly.

He answered with a brief silence, followed by a terse agreement. "I'll come to your room."

Dev thought he'd done a damned good job of conquering his fury over that business with the photographer. Yes, he'd let it get the better of him when he'd accused Sarah's magazine of staging her own abduction. And yes, he'd come on a little strong earlier this evening when she'd questioned whether he'd hold to his end of their agreement.

He'd had plenty of time to regret both lapses. She'd seen to that by slipping out of the hotel without him. The brief message she'd left while he was in the shower had pissed him off all over again.

Now she'd issued a summons in that aristocratic lady-of-the-manor tone. She'd better not try to shove the emerald at him again. Or deliver any more crap about their "arrangement" being over. They were long past the arrangement stage, and she knew it. She was just too stubborn to admit it.

She'd just have to accept that he wasn't perfect. He'd screwed up this afternoon by throwing that accusation at her. He'd apologize again. Crawl if he had to. Whatever it took, he intended to make it clear she wasn't rid of him. Not by a long shot.

That was the plan, anyway, right up until she opened the door. The mottled purple on her cheek tore the heart and the heat right out of him. Curling a knuckle, he brushed it gently across the skin below the bruise.

"Does this hurt as bad as it looks?"

"Not even close."

She didn't shy away from his touch. Dev took that as a hopeful sign. That, and the fact that some of the stiffness went out of her spine as she led him into the sitting area.

Nor did it escape his attention that she'd cut off the view that had so enchanted her before. The heavy, room-darkening drapes were drawn tight, blocking anyone from seeing out…or in.

"Would you like a drink?" she asked politely, gesturing to the well-stocked minibar.

"No, thanks, I'm good."

As he spoke, an image on the TV snagged his glance. The sound was muted but he didn't need it to recognize the amateur video playing across the screen. He'd already seen it several times.

Sarah noticed what had caught his attention and picked up the remote. "Have you seen the news coverage?"

"Yeah."

Clicking off the TV, she sank into an easy chair and raised a stockinged foot. Her arms locked around her bent knee and her green eyes regarded him steadily.

"I took your advice and thought more about our…our situation."

"That's one way to describe it," he acknowledged. "You come to any different conclusions about how we should handle it?"

"As a matter of fact, I did."

Dev waited, wanting to hear her thoughts.

"I feel as though I jumped on a speeding train. Everything happened so fast. You, me, Paris. Now Grandmama is insisting on…" She broke off, a flush rising, and took a moment to recover. "I was afraid the news services might pick up the kidnapping story, so I called her and tried to shrug off the incident as the work of bumbling amateurs."

"Did she buy that?"

"No."

"Smart woman, your grandmother."

"You might not agree when I tell you she segued immediately from that to insisting on a May wedding."

Well, what do you know? Dev was pretty sure he'd passed inspection with the duchess. Good to have it confirmed, especially since he apparently had a number of hurdles to overcome before he regained her granddaughter's trust.

"I repeat, your grandmother's a smart woman."

"She is, but then she doesn't know the facts behind our manufactured engagement."

"Do you think she needs to?"

"What I think," Sarah said slowly, "is that we need to put the brakes on this runaway train."

Putting the brakes on was a long step from her earlier insistence they call things off. Maybe he didn't face as many hurdles as he'd thought.

His tension easing by imperceptible degrees, Dev cocked his head. "How do you propose we do that?"

"We step back. Take some time to assess this attraction we both seem to…"

"Attraction?" He shook his head. "Sorry, sweetheart, I can't let you get away with that one. You and I both know we've left attraction in the dust."

"You're right."

She rested her chin on her knee, obviously searching for the right word. Impatience bit at him, but he reined it in. If he hadn't learned anything else today, he'd discovered Sarah could only be pushed so far.

"I won't lie," she said slowly. "What I feel for you is so different from anything I've ever experienced before. I think it's love. No, I'm pretty sure it's love."

That was all he needed to hear. He started toward her, but she stopped him with a quick palms-up gesture.

"What I'm *not* sure of, Dev, is whether love's enough to overcome the fact that we barely know each other."

"I know all I need to know about you."

"Oh. Right." She made a wry face. "I forgot about the background investigation."

He wouldn't apologize. He'd been up front with her about that. But he did attempt to put it in perspective.

"The investigation provided the externals, Sarah. The

time we've spent together, as brief as it's been, provided the essentials."

"Really?" She lifted a brow. "What's my favorite color? Am I a dog or a cat person? What kind of music do I like?"

"You consider those essentials?" he asked, genuinely curious.

"They're some of the bits and pieces that constitute the whole. Don't you think we should see how those pieces fit together before getting in any deeper?"

"I don't, but you obviously do."

If this was a business decision, he would ruthlessly override what he privately considered trivial objections. He'd made up his mind. He knew what he wanted.

Sarah did, too, apparently. With a flash of extremely belated insight, Dev realized she wanted to be courted. More to the point, she *deserved* to be courted.

Lady Sarah St. Sebastian might work at a magazine that promoted flashy and modern and ultrachic, but she held to old-fashioned values that he'd come to appreciate as much as her innate elegance and surprising sensuality. Her fierce loyalty to her sister, for instance. Her bone-deep love for the duchess. Her refusal to accept anything from him except her grandmother's emerald ring, and then only on a temporary basis.

He could do old-fashioned. He could do slow and courtly. Maybe. Admittedly, he didn't have a whole lot of experience in either. Moving out and taking charge came as natural to him as breathing. But if throttling back on his more aggressive instincts was what she wanted, that was what she'd get.

"Okay, we'll do it your way."

He started toward her again. Surprised and more than a little wary of his relatively easy capitulation, Sarah let her raised foot slip to the floor and pushed out of her chair.

He stopped less than a yard away. Close enough to kiss,

which she had to admit she wouldn't have minded all that much at this point. He settled for a touch instead. He kept it light, just a brush of his fingertips along the underside of her chin.

"We'll kick off phase two," he promised in a tone that edged toward deep and husky. "No negotiated contracts this time, no self-imposed deadlines. Just you and me, learning each other's little idiosyncrasies. If that's what you really want…?"

She nodded, although the soft dance of his fingers under her chin and the proximity of his mouth made it tough to stay focused.

"It's what I really want."

"All right, I'll call Patrick."

"Who? Oh, right. Your executive assistant. Excuse me for asking, but what does he have to do with this?"

"He's going to clear my calendar. Indefinitely. He'll blow every one of his fuses, but he'll get it done."

His fingers made another pass. Sarah's thoughts zinged wildly between the little pinpricks of pleasure he was generating and that "indefinitely."

"What about your schedule?" he asked. "How much time can you devote to phase two?"

"My calendar's wide-open, too. I quit my job."

"You didn't have to do that. I'm already past the business with the photographer."

"You may be," she retorted. "I'm not."

He absorbed that for a moment. "All right. Here's what we'll do, then. We give our statements to the *Brigade criminelle* at nine tomorrow morning and initiate phase two immediately after. Agreed?"

"Agreed."

"Good. I'll have a car waiting at eight-thirty to take us downtown. See you down in the lobby then."

He leaned in and brushed his lips over hers.

"Good night, Sarah."

She'd never really understood that old saying about being hoisted with your own petard. It had something to do with getting caught up in a medieval catapult, she thought. Or maybe hanging by one foot in a tangle of ropes from the mast of a fourteenth-century frigate.

Either situation would pretty much describe her feelings when Dev crossed the room and let himself out.

Thirteen

Sarah spent hours tossing and turning and kicking herself for her self-imposed celibacy. As a result, she didn't fall asleep until almost one and woke late the next morning.

The first thing she did was roll over in bed and grab her cell phone from the nightstand to check for messages. Still nothing from Gina, dammit, but Alexis had left two voice mails apologizing for what she termed an unfortunate misunderstanding and emphatically refusing to accept her senior layout editor's resignation.

"Misunderstanding, my ass."

Her mouth set, Sarah deleted the voice mails and threw back the covers. She'd have to hustle to be ready for the car Dev had said would be waiting at eight-thirty. A quick shower eliminated most of the cobwebs from her restless night. An equally quick cup of strong brew from the little coffeemaker in her room helped with the remainder.

Before she dressed, she stuck her nose through the balcony doors to assess the weather. No fog or drizzle, but still chilly enough to make her opt for her gray wool slacks and cherry-red sweater coat. She topped them with a scarf doubled around her throat European-style and a black beret tilted to a decidedly French angle.

She rushed down to the lobby with two minutes to spare and saw Dev had also prepared for the chill. But in jeans, a black turtleneck and a tan cashmere coat this morning instead of his usual business suit. He greeted her with a smile and a quick kiss.

"*Bonjour, ma chérie.* Sleep well?"

She managed not to wince at his accent. "Fairly well."

"Did you have time for breakfast?"

"No."

"I was running a little late, too, so I had the driver pick up some chocolate croissants and coffees. Shall we go?"

He offered his arm in a gesture she was beginning to realize was as instinctive as it was courteous. When she tucked her hand in the crook of his elbow, she could feel his warmth through the soft wool. Feel, too, the ripple of hard muscle as he leaned past her to push open the hotel door.

Traffic was its usual snarling beast, but the coffee and chocolate croissants mitigated the frustration. They were right on time when they pulled up at the block-long building overlooking the Seine that housed the headquarters of the *Brigade criminelle*. A lengthy sequence of security checkpoints, body scans and ID verification made them late for their appointment, however.

Detective Inspector Marie-Renée Delacroix waved aside their apologies as unnecessary and signed them in. Short and barrel-shaped, she wore a white blouse, black slacks and rubber-soled granny shoes. The semiautomatic nested in her shoulder holster belied her otherwise unprepossessing exterior.

"Thank you for coming in," she said in fluent English. "I'll try to make this as swift and painless as possible. Please, come with me."

She led them up a flight of stairs and down a long corridor interspersed with heavy oak doors. When Delacroix pushed through the door to her bureau, Sarah looked about with interest. The inspector's habitat didn't resemble the bull pens depicted on American TV police dramas. American bull pens probably didn't, either, she acknowledged wryly.

There were no dented metal file cabinets or half-empty cartons of doughnuts. No foam cups littering back-to-back desks or squawking phones. The area was spacious and well lit and smoke free. Soundproofing dividers offered at least the illusion of privacy, while monitors mounted high on the front wall flashed what looked like real-time updates on hot spots around Paris.

"Would you like coffee?" Delacroix asked as she waved them to seats in front of her desk.

Sarah looked to Dev before answering for them both. "No, thank you."

The inspector dropped into the chair behind the desk. Shoulders hunched, brows straight-lined, she dragged a wireless keyboard into reach and attacked it with two stubby forefingers. The assault was merciless, but for reasons known only to French computer gods, the typed versions of the statements Sarah and Dev had given to the responding officers wouldn't spit out of the printer.

"Merde!"

Muttering under her breath, she jabbed at the keyboard yet again. She looked as though she'd like to whip out her weapon and deliver a lethal shot when she finally admitted defeat and slammed away from her desk.

"Please wait. I need to find someone who can kick a report out of this piece of sh— Er, crap."

She returned a few moments later with a colleague in a blue-striped shirt and red suspenders. Without a word, he pressed a single key. When the printer began coughing up papers, he rolled his eyes and departed.

"I hate these things," Delacroix muttered as she dropped into her chair again.

Sarah and Dev exchanged a quick look but refrained from comment. Just as well, since the inspector became all brisk efficiency once the printer had disgorged the documents she wanted. She pushed two ink pens and the printed statements in their direction.

"Review these, please, and make any changes you feel necessary."

The reports were lengthy and correct. Delacroix was relieved that neither Sarah nor Dev had any changes, but consciously did her duty.

"Are you sure, mademoiselle? With that nasty bruise, we could add assault to the kidnapping charge."

Sarah fingered her cheek. Much as she'd like to double the case against Lefèvre, he hadn't directly caused the injury.

"I'm sure."

"Very well. Sign here, please, and here."

She did as instructed and laid down her pen. "You said you were going to talk to the prosecuting attorney about whether we need to remain in Paris for the arraignment," she reminded Delacroix.

"Ah, yes. He feels your statements, the evidence we've collected and the confessions from Lefèvre and his associate are more than sufficient for the case against them. As long as we know how to contact you and Monsieur Hunter if necessary, you may depart Paris whenever you wish."

Oddly, the knowledge that she could fly home at any time produced a contradictory desire in Sarah to remain in Paris for the initiation of phase two. That, and the way Dev once again tucked her arm in his as they descended the broad staircase leading to the main exit. There was still so much of the city—*her* city—she wanted to share with him.

The moment they stepped out into the weak sunshine, a blinding barrage of flashes sent Sarah stumbling back. Dismayed, she eyed the wolf pack crowding the front steps, their news vans parked at the curb behind them. While sound handlers thrust their boom mikes over the reporters' heads, the questions flew at Sarah like bullets. She heard her name and Dev's and Lefèvre's and Elise Girault's all seemingly in the same sentences.

She ducked her chin into her scarf and started to scramble back into police headquarters to search out a side exit. Dev stood his ground, though, and with her arm tucked tight against his side, Sarah had no choice but to do the same.

"Might as well give them what they want now," he told her. "Maybe it'll satisfy their appetites and send them chasing after their next victim."

Since most of the questions zinged at them were in French, Sarah found herself doing the translating and leaving the responding to Dev. He'd obviously fielded these kinds of rapid-fire questions before. He deftly avoided any that might impact the case against the kidnappers and confirmed only that he and Sarah were satisfied with the way the police were handling the matter.

The questions soon veered from the official to the personal. To Sarah's surprise, Dev shelved his instinctive dislike of the media and didn't cut them off at the knees. His responses were concise and to the point.

Yes, he and Lady Sarah had only recently become engaged. Yes, they'd known each other only a short time. No, they hadn't yet set a date for the wedding.

"Although," he added with a sideways glance at Sarah, "her grandmother has voiced some thoughts in that regard."

"Speaking of the duchess," a sharp-featured reporter commented as she thrust her mike almost in Sarah's face, "Charlotte St. Sebastian was once the toast of Paris and New York. From all reports, she's now penniless. Have you insisted Monsieur Hunter include provisions for her maintenance in your prenup agreement?"

Distaste curled Sarah's lip but she refused to give the

vulture any flesh to feed on. "As my fiancé has just stated," she said with a dismissive smile, "we've only recently become engaged. And what better place to celebrate that engagement than Paris, the City of Lights and Love? So now you must excuse us, as that's what we intend to do."

She tugged on Dev's arm and he took the hint. When they cleared the mob and started for the limo waiting a half block away, he gave her a curious look.

"What was that all about?"

She hadn't translated the last question and would prefer not to now. Their engagement had been tumultuous enough. Despite her grandmother's insistence on booking the Plaza, Sarah hadn't really thought as far ahead as marriage. Certainly not as far as a prenup.

They stopped beside the limo. The driver had the door open and waiting but Dev waved him back inside the car.

"Give us a minute here, Andre."

"*Oui*, monsieur."

While the driver slid into the front seat, Dev angled Sarah to face him. Her shoulders rested against the rear door frame. Reluctantly, she tipped up her gaze to meet his.

"You might as well tell me," he said. "I'd rather not be blindsided by hearing whatever it was play on the five-o'clock news."

"The reporter wanted details on our prenup." She hunched her shoulders, feeling awkward and embarrassed. "I told her to get stuffed."

His grin broke out, quick and slashing. "In your usual elegant manner, of course."

"Of course."

Still grinning, he studied her face. It must have reflected her acute discomfort because he stooped to speak to the driver.

"We've decided to walk, Andre. We won't need you anymore today."

When the limo eased away from the curb, he hooked

Sarah's arm through his again and steered her into the stream of pedestrians.

"I know how prickly you are about the subject of finances, so we won't go there until we've settled more important matters, like whether you're a dog or cat person. Which are you, by the way?"

"Dog," she replied, relaxing for the first time that morning. "The bigger the better, although the only one we've ever owned was the Pomeranian that Gina brought home one day. She was eight or nine at the time and all indignant because someone had left it leashed outside a coffee shop in one-hundred-degree heat."

Too late she realized she might have opened the door for Dev to suggest Gina had developed kleptomaniac tendencies early. She glanced up, met his carefully neutral look and hurried on with her tale.

"We went back and tried to find the owner, but no one would claim it. We soon found out why. Talk about biting the hand that feeds you! The nasty little beast snapped and snarled and wouldn't let anyone pet him except Grandmama."

"No surprise there. The duchess has a way about her. She certainly cowed me."

"Right," Sarah scoffed. "I saw how you positively quaked in her presence."

"I'm still quaking. Finish the story. What happened to the beast?"

"Grandmama finally palmed him off on an acquaintance of hers. What about you?" she asked, glancing up at him again. "Do you prefer dogs or cats?"

"Bluetick coonhounds," he answered without hesitation. "Best hunters in the world. We had a slew of barn cats, though. My sisters were always trying to palm their litters off on friends, too."

Intrigued, Sarah pumped him for more details about

his family. "I know you grew up on a ranch. In Nebraska, wasn't it?"

"New Mexico, but it was more like a hardscrabble farm than a ranch."

"Do your parents still work the farm?"

"They do. They like the old place and have no desire to leave it, although they did let me make a few improvements."

More than a few, Sarah guessed.

"What about your sisters?"

He had four, she remembered, none of whom had agreed to be interviewed for the *Beguile* article. The feeling that their business was nobody else's ran deep in the Hunter clan.

"All married, all comfortable, all happy. You hungry?"

The abrupt change of subject threw Sarah off until she saw what had captured his attention. They'd reached the Pont de l'Alma, which gave a bird's-eye view of the glass-roofed barges docked on the north side of the Seine. One boat was obviously set for a lunch cruise. Its linen-draped tables were set with gleaming silver and crystal.

"Have you ever taken one of these Seine river cruises?" Dev asked.

"No."

"Why not?"

"They're, uh, a little touristy."

"This is Paris. Everyone's a tourist, even the Parisians."

"Good God, don't let a native hear you say that!"

"What do you say? Want to mingle with the masses for a few hours?"

She threw a glance at a tour bus disgorging its load of passengers and swallowed her doubts.

"I'm game if you are."

He steered her to the steps that led down to the quay. Sarah fully expected them to be turned away at the ticket office. While a good number of boats cruised the Seine, picking up or letting off passengers at various stops, tour agencies tended to book these lunch and dinner cruises for large groups months in advance.

Whatever Dev said—or paid—at the ticket booth not only got them on the boat, it garnered a prime table for two beside the window. Their server introduced herself and filled their aperitif glasses with kir. A smile in his eyes, Dev raised his glass.

"To us."

"To us," Sarah echoed softly.

The cocktail went down with velvet smoothness. She savored the intertwined flavors while Dev gave his glass a respectful glance.

"What's in this?"

"*Crème de cassis*—black-currant liqueur—topped with white wine. It's named for Félix Kir, the mayor of Dijon, who popularized the drink after World War II."

"Well, it doesn't have the same wallop as your grandmother's *Žuta Osa* but it's good."

"'Scuse me."

The interruption came from the fortyish brunette at the next table. She beamed Sarah a friendly smile.

"Y'all are Americans, aren't you?"

"Yes, we are."

"So are we. We're the Parkers. Evelyn and Duane Parker, from Mobile."

Sarah hesitated. She hated to be rude, but Evelyn's leopard-print Versace jacket and jewel-toed boots indicated she kept up with the latest styles. If she read *Beguile,* she would probably recognize Number Three from the Sexiest Singles article. Or from the recent news coverage.

Dev solved her dilemma by gesturing to the cell phone Evelyn clutched in one hand. "I'm Dev and this is my fiancée, Sarah. Would you like me to take a picture of you and your husband?"

"Please. And I'll do one of y'all."

The accordion player began strolling the aisle while cell phones were still being exchanged and photos posed for. When he broke into a beautiful baritone, all conversation on the boat ceased and Sarah breathed easy again.

Moments later, they pulled away from the dock and glided under the first of a dozen or more bridges yet to come. Meal service began then. Sarah wasn't surprised at the quality of the food. This was Paris, after all. She and Dev sampled each of the starters: foie gras on a toasted baguette; Provençal smoked salmon and shallots; duck magret salad with cubes of crusty goat cheese; tiny vegetable egg rolls fried to a pale golden brown. Sarah chose honey-and-sesame-seed pork tenderloin for her main dish. Dev went with the veal blanquette. With each course, their server poured a different wine. Crisp, chilled whites. Medium reds. Brandy with the rum baba they each selected for dessert.

Meanwhile, Paris's most famous monuments were framed in the windows. The Louvre. La Conciergerie. Notre Dame. The Eiffel Tower.

The boat made a U-turn while Sarah and Dev lingered over coffee, sharing more of their pasts. She listened wide-eyed to the stories Dev told of his Air Force days. She suspected he edited them to minimize the danger and maximize the role played by others on his crew. Still, the war-torn countries he'd flown into and the horrific disasters he'd helped provide lifesaving relief for made her world seem frivolous by comparison.

"Grandmama took us abroad every year," she related when he insisted it was her turn. "She was determined to expose Gina and me to cultures other than our own."

"Did she ever take you to Karlenburgh?"

"No, never. That would have been too painful for her. I'd like to go someday, though. We still have cousins there, three or four times removed."

She traced a fingertip around the rim of her coffee cup.

Although it tore at her pride, she forced herself to admit the truth.

"Gina and I never knew what sacrifices Grandmama had to make to pay for those trips. Or for my year at the Sorbonne."

"I'm guessing your sister still doesn't know."

She jerked her head up, prepared to defend Gina yet again. But there was nothing judgmental in Dev's expression. Only quiet understanding.

"She has a vague idea," Sarah told him. "I never went into all the gory details, but she's not stupid."

Dev had to bite down on the inside of his lower lip. Eugenia Amalia Thérése St. Sebastian hadn't impressed him with either her intelligence or her common sense. Then again, he hadn't been particularly interested in her intellectual prowess the few times they'd connected.

In his defense, few horny, heterosexual males could see beyond Gina's stunning beauty. At least not until they'd spent more than an hour or two in the bubbleheaded blonde's company. Deciding discretion was the better part of valor, he chose not to share that particular observation.

He couldn't help comparing the sisters, though. No man in his right mind would deny that he'd come out the winner in the St. Sebastian lottery. Charm, elegance, smarts, sensuality and...

He'd better stop right there! When the hell had he reached the point where the mere thought of Sarah's smooth, sleek body stretched out under his got him rock hard? Where the memory of how she'd opened her legs for him damned near steamed up the windows beside their table?

Suddenly Dev couldn't wait for the boat to pass under the last bridge. By the time they'd docked and he'd hustled Sarah up the gangplank, his turtleneck was strangling him. The look of confused concern she flashed at him as they climbed the steps to street level didn't help matters.

"Are you all right?"

He debated for all of two seconds before deciding on the truth. "Not anywhere close to all right."

"Oh, no! Was it the foie gras?" Dismayed, she rushed to the curb to flag down a cab. "You have to be careful with goose liver."

"Sarah…"

"I should have asked if it had been wrapped in grape leaves and slow cooked. That's the safest method."

"Sarah…"

A cab screeched to the curb. Forehead creased with worry, she yanked on the door handle. Dev had to wait until they were in the taxi and heading for the hotel to explain his sudden incapacitation.

"It wasn't the foie gras."

Concern darkened her eyes to deep, verdant green. "The veal, then? Was it bad?"

"No, sweetheart. It's you."

"I beg your pardon?"

Startled, she lurched back against her seat. Dev cursed his clumsiness and hauled her into his arms.

"As delicious as lunch was, all I could think about was how you taste." His mouth roamed hers. His voice dropped to a rough whisper. "How you fit against me. How you arch your back and make that little noise in your throat when you're about to climax."

She leaned back in his arms. She wanted him as much as he wanted her. He could see it in the desire that shaded her eyes to deep, dark emerald. In the way her breath had picked up speed. Fierce satisfaction knifed into him. She was rethinking the cooling-off period, Dev thought exultantly. She had to recognize how unnecessary this phase two was.

His hopes took a nosedive—and his respect for Sarah's

willpower kicked up a grudging notch—when she drew in
a shuddering breath and gave him a rueful smile.

"Well, I'm glad it wasn't the goose liver."

Fourteen

As the cab rattled along the quay, Sarah wondered how she could be such a blithering idiot. One word from her, just one little word, and she could spend the rest of the afternoon and evening curled up with Dev in bed. Or on the sofa. Or on cushions tossed onto the floor in front of the fire, or in the shower, soaping his back and belly, or…

She leaned forward, her gaze suddenly snagged by the green bookstalls lining the riverside of the boulevard. And just beyond the stalls, almost directly across from the renowned bookstore known as Shakespeare and Company, was a familiar bridge.

"Stop! We'll get out here!"

The command surprised both Dev and the cabdriver, but he obediently pulled over to the curb and Dev paid him off.

"Your favorite bookstore?" he asked with a glance at the rambling, green-fronted facade of the shop that specialized in English-language books. Opened in 1951, the present store had assumed the mantle of the original Shakespeare and Company, a combination bookshop, lending library and haven for writers established in 1917 by American expatriate Sylvia Beach and frequented by the likes of Ernest Hemingway, Ezra Pound and F. Scott Fitzgerald. During her year at the Sorbonne, Sarah had loved exploring the shelves crammed floor to ceiling in the shop's small, crowded rooms. She'd never slept in one of the thirteen beds available to indigent students or visitors who just wanted to sleep in the rarified literary atmosphere, but she'd hunched for hours at the tables provided for scholars, researchers and book lovers of all ages.

It wasn't Shakespeare and Company that had snagged her eye, though. It was the bridge just across the street from it.

"That's the Archbishop's Bridge," she told Dev with a smile that tinged close to embarrassment.

She'd always considered herself the practical sister, too levelheaded to indulge in the kind of extravagant flights of fancy that grabbed Gina. Yet she'd just spent several delightful hours on a touristy, hopelessly romantic river cruise. Why not cap that experience with an equally touristy romantic gesture?

"Do you see these locks?" she asked as she and Dev crossed the street and approached the iron bridge.

"Hard to miss 'em," he drawled, eyeing the almost solid wall of brass obscuring the bridge's waist-high grillwork. "What's the story here?"

"I'm told it's a recent fad that's popping up on all the bridges of Paris. People ascribe wishes or dreams to locks and fasten them to the bridge, then throw the key in the river."

Dev stooped to examine some of the colorful ribbons, charms and printed messages dangling from various locks. "Here's a good one. This couple from Dallas wish their kids great joy, but don't plan to produce any additional offspring. Evidently seven are enough."

"Good grief! Seven would be enough for me, too."

"Really?"

He straightened and leaned a hip against the rail. The breeze ruffled his black hair and tugged at the collar of his camel-hair sport coat.

"I guess that's one of those little idiosyncrasies we should find out about each other, almost as important as whether we prefer dogs or cats. How many kids *do* you want, Sarah?"

"I don't know." She trailed a finger over the oblong hasp of a bicycle lock. "Two, at least, although I wouldn't mind three or even four."

As impulsive and thoughtless as Gina could be at times, Sarah couldn't imagine growing up without the joy of her bubbly laugh and warm, generous personality.

"How about you?" she asked Dev. "How many offspring would you like to produce?"

"Well, my sisters contend that the number of kids their husbands want is inversely proportional to how many stinky diapers they had to change. I figure I can manage a couple of rounds of diapers. Three or maybe even four if I get the hang of it."

He nodded to the entrepreneur perched on his overturned crate at the far end of the bridge. The man's pegboard full of locks gleamed dully in the afternoon sun.

"What do you think? Should we add a wish that we survive stinky diapers to the rest of these hopes and dreams?"

Still a little embarrassed by her descent into sappy sentimentality, Sarah nodded. She waited on the bridge while Dev purchased a hefty lock. Together they scouted for an open spot. She found one two-thirds of the way across the bridge, but Dev hesitated before attaching his purchase.

"We need to make it more personal." Frowning, he eyed the bright ribbons and charms dangling from so many of the other locks. "We need a token or something to scribble on."

He patted the pockets of his sport coat and came up

with the ticket stubs from their lunch cruise. "How about one of these?"

"That works. The cruise gave me a view of Paris I'd never seen before. I'm glad I got to share it with you, Dev."

Busy scribbling on the back of a ticket, he merely nodded. Sarah was a little surprised by his offhanded acceptance of her tribute until she read what he'd written.

To our two or three or four or more kids,
we promise you one cruise each on the Seine.

"And I thought *I* was being mushy and sentimental," she said, laughing.

"Mushy and sentimental is what phase two is all about." Unperturbed, he punched the hasp through the ticket stub. "Here, you attach it."

When the lock clicked into place, Sarah knew she'd always remember this moment. Rising up on tiptoe, she slid her arms around Dev's neck.

She'd remember the kiss, too. Particularly when Dev valiantly stuck to their renegotiated agreement later that evening.

After their monster lunch, they opted for supper at a pizzeria close to the Hôtel Verneuil. One glass of red wine and two mushroom-and-garlic slices later, they walked back to the hotel through a gray, soupy fog. Monsieur LeBon had gone off duty, but the receptionist on the desk relayed his shock over the news of the attack on Lady Sarah and his profound regret that she had suffered such an indignity while in Paris.

Sarah smiled her thanks and made a mental note to speak to the manager personally tomorrow. Once on her floor, she slid the key card into her room lock and slanted Dev a questioning look.

"Do you want to come in for a drink?"

"A man can only endure so much torture." His expression rueful, he traced a knuckle lightly over the bruise she'd already forgotten. "Unless you're ready to initiate phase three, we'd better call it a night."

She was ready. More than ready. But the companionship she and Dev had shared after leaving Inspector Delacroix's office had delivered as much punch as the hours they'd spent tangled up in the sheets. A different kind of punch, admittedly. Emotional rather than physical, but every bit as potent.

Although she knew she'd regret it the moment she closed the door, Sarah nodded. "Let's give phase two a little more time."

She was right. She did regret it. But she decided the additional hours she spent curled up on the sofa watching very boring TV were appropriate punishment for being so stupid. She loved Dev. He obviously loved her. Why couldn't she just trust her instincts and…

The buzz of her cell phone cut into her disgusted thoughts. She reached for the instrument, half hoping it was Alexis trying to reach her again. Sarah was in the mood to really, really unload on her ex-boss. When her sister's picture flashed up on the screen, she almost dropped the phone in her excitement and relief.

"Gina! Where are you?"

"Lucerne. I…I waited until morning in New York to call you but…"

"I'm not in New York. I'm in Paris, as you would know if you'd bothered to answer any of my calls."

"Thank God!"

The moaned exclamation startled her, but not as much as the sobs her sister suddenly broke into. Sarah lurched upright on the sofa, the angry tirade she'd intended to deliver instantly forgotten.

"What's wrong? Gina! What's happened?"

A dozen different disasters flooded into her mind. Gina had taken a tumble on the ski slopes. Broken a leg or an arm. Or her neck. She could be paralyzed. Breathing by machine.

"Are you hurt?" she demanded, fear icing her heart. "Gina, are you in the hospital?"

"Nooo."

The low wail left her limp with relief. In almost the next heartbeat, panic once again fluttered like a trapped bird inside her chest. She could count on the fingers of one hand the times she'd heard her always-upbeat, always-sunny sister cry.

"Sweetie, talk to me. Tell me what's wrong."

"I can't. Not...not over the phone. Please come, Sarah. *Please!* I need you."

It didn't even occur to her to say no. "I'll catch the next flight to Lucerne. Tell me where you're staying."

"The Rebstock."

"The hotel Grandmama took us to the summer you turned fourteen?"

That set off another bout of noisy, hiccuping sobs. "Don't...don't tell Grandmama about this."

About *what?* Somehow, Sarah choked back the shout and offered a soothing promise.

"I won't. Just keep your phone on, Gina. I'll call you as soon as I know when I can get there."

She cut the connection, switched to the phone's internet browser and pulled up a schedule of flights from Paris to Lucerne. Her pulse jumped when she found a late-night shuttle to Zurich that departed Charles de Gaulle Airport at 11:50 p.m. From there she'd have to rent a car and drive the sixty-five kilometers to Lake Lucerne.

She could make the flight. She had to make it. Her heart racing, she reserved a seat and scrambled off the sofa. She started for the bedroom to throw some things together but made a quick detour to the sitting room desk and snatched up the house phone.

"Come on, Dev. Answer!"

Her quivering nerves stretched tighter as it rang six times, then cut to the hotel operator.

"May I help you, Lady Sarah?"

"I'm trying to reach Monsieur Hunter, but he doesn't answer."

"May I take a message for you?"

"Yes, please. Tell him to call me as soon as possible."

Hell! Where was he?

Slamming the phone down, she dashed into the bedroom. She didn't have time to pack. Just shove her laptop in her shoulder tote, grab her sweater coat, make sure her purse held her passport and credit cards and run.

While the elevator made its descent, she tried to reach Dev by cell phone. She'd just burst into the lobby when he answered on a husky, teasing note.

"Please tell me you've decided to put me out of my misery."

"Where are you?" The phone jammed to her ear, she rushed through the lobby. "I called your room but there wasn't any answer.

"I couldn't sleep. I went out for a walk." He caught the tension in her voice. The teasing note dropped out of his. "Why? What's up?"

"Gina just called."

"It's about time."

She pushed through the front door. The fog had cleared, thank God, and several taxis still cruised the streets. She waved a frantic arm to flag one down, the phone clutched in her other fist.

"She's in some kind of trouble, Dev."

"So what else is new?"

If she hadn't been so worried, the sarcastic comment might not have fired her up as hot and fast as it did.

"Spare me the editorial," she snapped back angrily. "My sister needs me. I'm on my way to Switzerland."

"Whoa! Hold on a minute…"

The taxi rolled up to the curb. She jumped in and issued a terse order. "De Gaulle Airport. Hurry, please."

"Dammit, Sarah, I can't be more than ten or fifteen minutes from the hotel. Wait until I get back and we'll sort this out together."

"She's *my* sister. I'll sort it out." She was too rushed and too torqued by his sarcasm to measure her words. "I'll call you as soon as I know what's what."

"Yeah," he bit out, as pissed off now as she was. "You do that."

In no mood to soothe his ruffled feathers, she cut the connection and leaned into the Plexiglas divider.

"I need to catch an eleven-fifty flight," she told the cab-driver. "There's an extra hundred francs in it for you if I make it."

The Swiss Air flight was only half-full. Most of the passengers looked like businessmen who wanted to be on scene when Zurich's hundreds of banks opened for business in the morning. There were a few tourists scattered among them, and several students with crammed backpacks getting a jump start on spring break in the Alps.

Sarah stared out the window through most of the ninety-minute flight. The inky darkness beyond the strobe lights on the wing provided no answers to the worried questions tumbling through her mind.

Was it the ski instructor? Had he left Gina stranded in Lucerne? Or Dev's Byzantine medallion? Had she tried to sell it and smacked up against some law against peddling antiquities on the black market?

Her stomach was twisted into knots by the time they landed in Zurich, and she rushed to the airport's Europcar desk. Fifteen minutes later she was behind the wheel of a rented Peugeot and zipping out of the airport. Once she hit the main motorway, she fumbled her phone out of her purse and speed-dialed her sister.

"I just landed in Zurich," Sarah informed her. "I'm in a rental car and should be there within an hour."

"Okay. Thanks for coming, Sarah. I'll call down to reception and tell them to expect you."

To her profound relief, Gina sounded much calmer. Probably because she knew the cavalry was on the way.

"I'll see you shortly."

Once Sarah left the lights of Zurich behind, she zoomed south on the six-lane E41. Speed limits in Switzerland didn't approach the insanity of those in Germany, but the 120 kilometers per hour max got her to the shores of Lake Lucerne in a little over forty minutes.

The city of Lucerne sat on the western arm of the lake. A modern metropolis with an ancient center, its proximity to the Alps had made it a favorite destination for tourists from the earliest days of the Hapsburg Empire. The Duchy of Karlenburgh had once constituted a minuscule part of that vast Hapsburg empire. As the lights of the city glowed in the distance, Sarah remembered that Grandmama had shared some of the less painful stories from the St. Sebastians' past during their stay in Lucerne.

She wasn't thinking of the past as she wound through the narrow streets of the Old Town. Only of her sister and whether whatever trouble Gina was in might impact their grandmother's health. The old worries she'd carried for so long—the worries she'd let herself slough off when she'd gotten so tangled up with Dev—came crashing back.

It was almost 3:00 a.m. when she pulled up at the entrance to the Hotel zum Rebstock. Subdued lighting illuminated its half-timbered red-and-white exterior. Three stories tall, with a turreted tower anchoring one end of the building, the hotel had a history dating back to the 1300s.

Even this early in the season, geraniums filled its window boxes and ivy-covered trellises defined the tiny terrace that served as an outdoor restaurant and *biergarten*.

Weary beyond words, Sarah grabbed her tote and purse and left the car parked on the street. She'd have a valet move it to the public garage on the next block tomorrow. Right now all she cared about was getting to her sister.

As promised, Gina had notified reception of a late arrival. Good thing, since a sign on the entrance informed guests that for safety purposes a key card was required for entry after midnight. A sleepy attendant answered Sarah's knock and welcomed her to the Rebstock.

"Lady Eugenia asked that we give you a key. She is in room 212. The elevator is just down the hall. Or you may take the stairs."

"Thank you."

She decided the stairs would be quicker and would also work out the kinks in her back from the flight and the drive. The ancient wooden stairs creaked beneath their carpeted runner. So did the boards of the second-floor hallway as Sarah counted room numbers until she reached the one at the far end of the hall. A corner turret room, judging by the way its door was wedged between two others.

She slid the key card into the lock and let herself into a narrow, dimly lit entryway.

"Gina?"

The door whooshed shut behind her. Sarah rounded the corner of the entryway, found herself in a charming bedroom with a sitting area occupying the octagonal turret and came to a dead stop. Her sister was tucked under the double bed's downy duvet, sound asleep.

A rueful smile curved Sarah's lips. She'd raced halfway across Europe in response to a desperate plea. Yet whatever was troubling Gina didn't appear to be giving her nightmares. She lay on one side, curled in a tight ball with a hand under her cheek and her blond curls spilling across the pillow.

Shaking her head in amused affection, Sarah dropped her tote and purse on the sofa in the sitting area and plunked down on the side of the bed.

"Hey!" She poked her sister in the shoulder. "Wake up!"

"Huh?" Gina raised her head and blinked open blurry eyes. "Oh, good," she muttered, her voice thick with sleep. "You made it."

"Finally."

"You've got to be totally wiped," she mumbled. Scooting over a few inches, she dragged up a corner of the comforter. "Crawl in."

"Oh, for…!"

Sarah swallowed the rest of the exasperated exclamation. Gina's head had already plopped back to the pillow. Her lids fluttered shut and her raised arm sank like a stone.

The elder sister sat on the edge of the bed for a few moments longer, caught in a wash of relief and bone-deep love for the younger. Then she got up long enough to kick off her boots and unbelt the cherry-red sweater coat. Shrugging it off, she slid under the comforter.

As exhausted as she was from her frantic dash across Europe, it took Sarah longer than she would have believed possible to fall asleep. She lay in the half darkness, listening to her sister's steady breathing, trying yet again to guess what had sparked her panic. Gradually, her thoughts shifted to Dev and their last exchange.

She'd overreacted to his criticism of Gina. She knew that now. At the time, though, her one driving thought had been to get to the airport. She'd apologize tomorrow. He had sisters of his own. Surely he'd understand.

Fifteen

Sarah came awake to blinding sunshine and the fuzziness that results from too little sleep. She rolled over, grimacing at the scratchy pull of her slept-in slacks and turtleneck, and squinted at the empty spot beside her.

No Gina.

And no note, she discovered when she crawled out of bed and checked the sunny sitting room. More than a little annoyed, she padded into the bathroom. Face scrubbed, she appropriated her sister's hairbrush and found a complimentary toothbrush in the basket of amenities provided by the hotel.

Luckily, she and Gina wore the same size, if not the same style. While she was content to adapt her grandmother's vintage classics, her sister preferred a trendier, splashier look. Sarah raided Gina's underwear for a pair of silky black hipsters and matching demibra, then wiggled into a chartreuse leotard patterned in a wild Alice In Wonderland motif. She topped them with a long-sleeved, thigh-skimming wool jumper in electric blue and a three-inch-wide elaborately studded belt that rode low on her hips.

No way was she wearing her red sweater coat with these

eye-popping colors. She'd look like a clown-school dropout. She flicked a denim jacket off a hangar instead, hitched her purse over her shoulder and went in search of her sister.

She found Gina outside on the terrace, chatting with an elderly couple at the next table. She'd gathered her blond curls into a one-sided cascade and looked impossibly chic in pencil-legged jeans, a shimmering metallic tank and a fur-trimmed Michael Kors blazer. When she spotted Sarah, she jumped up and rushed over with her arms outstretched.

"You're finally up! You got in so late last night I... Omigod! What happened to your face?"

Sarah was more anxious to hear her sister's story than tell her own. "I got crosswise of a metal strut."

"I'm so sorry! Does it hurt?"

"Not anymore."

"Thank goodness. We'll have to cover it with foundation when we go back upstairs. Do you want some coffee?"

"God, yes!"

Sarah followed her back to the table and smiled politely when Gina introduced her to the elderly couple. They were from Düsseldorf, were both retired schoolteachers and had three children, all grown now.

"They've been coming to Lake Lucerne every spring for forty-seven years to celebrate their anniversary," Gina related as she filled a cup from the carafe on her table. "Isn't that sweet?"

"Very sweet."

Sarah splashed milk into the cup and took two, quick lifesaving gulps while Gina carried on a cheerful conversation with the teachers. As she listened to the chatter, Sarah began to feel much like the tumbling, upside-down Alices on the leotard. Had she fallen down some rabbit hole? Imagined the panic in her sister's voice last night? Dreamed the sobs?

The unreal feeling persisted until Gina saw that she'd downed most of her coffee. "I told the chambermaid to wait until you were up to do the room. She's probably in there now. Why don't we take a walk and...and talk?"

The small stutter and flicker of nervousness told Sarah she hadn't entered some alternate universe. With a smile for the older couple, Gina pushed her chair back. Sarah did the same.

"Let's go down to Chapel Bridge," she suggested. "We can talk there."

The Rebstock sat directly across the street from Lucerne's centuries-old Church of Leodegar, named for the city's patron saint. Just beyond the needle-spired church, the cobbled street angled downward, following the Reuss River as it flowed into the impossibly blue lake. Since the Reuss bisected the city, Lucerne could claim almost as many bridges as Venice. The most famous of them was the Chapel Bridge, or *Kapellbrücke*. Reputed to be the oldest covered wooden bridge in Europe, it was constructed in the early 1300s. Some sections had to be rebuilt after a 1993 fire supposedly sparked by a discarded cigarette. But the octagonal watchtower halfway across was original, and the window boxes filled with spring flowers made it a favorite meandering spot for locals and tourists alike.

Zigzagging for more than six hundred feet across the river, it was decorated with paintings inside that depicted Lucerne's history and offered wooden benches with stunning views of the town, the lake and the snowcapped Alps. Gina sank onto a bench some yards from the watchtower. Sarah settled beside her and waited while her sister gnawed on her lower lip and stared at the snowy peaks in uncharacteristic silence.

"You might as well tell me," she said gently after several moments. "Whatever's happened, we'll find a way to fix it."

Gina exhaled a long, shuddering breath. Twisting around on the bench, she reached for Sarah's hands.

"That's the problem. I came here to fix it. But at the last minute, I couldn't go through with it."

"Go through with what?"

"Terminating the pregnancy."

Sarah managed not to gasp or groan or mangle the fingers entwined with hers, but it took a fierce struggle.

"You're pregnant?"

"Barely. I peed on the stick even before I missed my period. I thought... I was sure we were safe. He wore a condom." She gave a short, dry laugh. "Actually, we went through a whole box of condoms that weekend."

"For God's sake, I don't need the details. Except maybe his name. I assume we're talking about your ski instructor."

"Who?"

"The cuddly ski instructor you texted me about."

"Oh. There isn't any ski instructor. I just needed an excuse for my sudden trip to Switzerland."

That arrowed straight to Sarah's heart. Never, *ever* would she have imagined that her sister would keep a secret like this from her.

"Oh, Gina, why did you need an excuse? Why didn't you just tell me about the baby?"

"I couldn't. You've been so worried about Grandmama and the doctor bills. I couldn't dump this problem on you, too."

She crunched Sarah's fingers, tears shimmering in her eyes.

"But last night... After I canceled my appointment at the clinic...it all sort of came down on me. I had to call you, had to talk to you. Then, when I heard your voice, I just lost it."

When she burst into wrenching sobs, Sarah wiggled a hand free of her bone-crushing grip and threw an arm around her.

"I'm *glad* you lost it," she said fiercely as Gina cried into her shoulder. "I'm *glad* I was close enough to come when you needed me."

They rocked together, letting the tears flow, until Gina finally raised a tear-streaked face.

"You okay?" Sarah asked, fishing a tissue out of her purse.

"No, but...but I will be."

Thank God. She heard the old Gina in that defiant sniff. She handed her the tissue and hid a grin when her sister honked like a Canadian goose.

"I meant to ask you about that, Sarah."

"About what?"

"How you could get here so fast. What were you doing in Paris?"

"I'll tell you later. Let's focus on you right now. And the baby. Who's the father, Gina, and does he know he is one?"

"Yes, to the second part. I was so wigged-out last night, I called him before I called you." She scrunched up her nose. "He didn't take it well."

"Bastard!"

"And then some." Her tears completely gone now, Gina gave an indignant sniff. "You wouldn't believe how obnoxious and overbearing he is. And I can't believe I fell for him, even for one weekend. Although in my defense, he gives new meaning to the phrase sex on the hoof."

"Who *is* this character?"

"No one you know. I met him in L.A. My company catered a party for him."

The bottom dropped out of Sarah's stomach. She could have sworn she heard it splat into the weathered boards. She stared at the snow-covered peaks in the distance, but all she could see was the surveillance video of Gina. At Dev's house in L.A. Catering a private party.

"What's...?" She dragged her tongue over suddenly dry lips. Her voice sounded hollow in her ears, as though it came from the bottom of a well. "What's his name?"

"Jack Mason." Gina's lip curled. "Excuse me, John Harris Mason, the third."

For a dizzying moment, Sarah couldn't catch her breath. She only half heard the diatribe her sister proceeded to pour out concerning the man. She caught that he was some kind of ambassador, however, and that he worked out of the State Department.

"How in the world did you hook up with someone from the State Department?"

"He was in L.A. for a benefit. A friend introduced us."

"Oh. Well…"

Since Gina seemed to have finally run out of steam, Sarah asked if she'd eaten breakfast.

"No, I was waiting for you to wake up."

"The baby…" She gestured at her sister's still-flat stomach. "You need to eat, and I'm starved. Why don't you go back to the hotel and order us a gargantuan breakfast? I'll join you after I make a few calls."

"You're not going to call Grandmama?" Alarm put a squeak in Gina's voice. "We can't drop this on her long-distance."

"Good Lord, no! I need to call Paris. I raced out so fast last night, I didn't pack my things or check out of the hotel."

Or wait for Dev to hotfoot it back to the Hôtel Verneuil. Sarah didn't regret that hasty decision. She wouldn't have made the Swiss Air flight if she'd waited. But she did regret the anger that had flared between them.

No need to tell Gina about Dev right now. Not when she and Sarah were both still dealing with the emotional whammy of her pregnancy. She'd tell her later, after things had calmed down a bit.

Which was why she waited until her sister was almost to the exit of the wooden tunnel to whip out her phone. And why frustration put a scowl on her face when Dev didn't answer his cell.

She left a brief message. Just a quick apology for her spurt of temper last night and a request for him to return her call as soon as possible. She started to slip the phone back into her purse, but decided to try his hotel room. The house phone rang six times before switching to the hotel operator, as it had last night.

"May I help you?"

"This is Sarah St. Sebastian. I'm trying to reach Monsieur Hunter."

"I'm sorry, Lady Sarah. Monsieur Hunter has checked out."

"What! When?"

"Early this morning. He told Monsieur LeBon an urgent business matter had come up at home that required his immediate attention. He also instructed us to hold your room for you until you return."

For the second time in less than ten minutes, Sarah's stomach took a dive.

"Did he...? Did he leave a message for me?"

"No, ma'am."

"Are you sure?"

"Quite sure, ma'am."

"I see. Thank you."

The hand holding the phone dropped to her lap. Once again she stared blindly at the dazzling white peak. Long moments later, she gave her head a little shake and pushed off the bench.

Gina needed her. They'd work on her problem first. Then, maybe, work on Sarah's. When she was calmer and could put this business with Dev in some kind of perspective.

The scene that greeted her when she walked into the Rebstock's lobby did nothing to promote a sense of calm. If anything, she was jolted into instant outrage by the sight of a tawny-haired stranger brutally gripping one of Gina's wrists. She was hammering at him with her free fist. The receptionist dithered ineffectually behind the counter.

"What are you doing?"

Sarah flew across the lobby, her hands curled into talons. She attacked from the side while Gina continued to assault the front. Between them, they forced the stranger to hunch his shoulders and shield his face from fifteen painted, raking fingernails.

"Hey! Back off, lady."

"Let her go!"

Sarah got in a vicious swipe that drew blood. The man, whom she now suspected was the overbearing, obnoxious ambassador, cursed.

"Jesus! Back off, I said!"

"Not until you let Gina go."

"The hell I will! She's got some explaining to do, and I'm not letting her out of my sight until..."

He broke off, as startled as Sarah when she was thrust aside by 180 pounds of savage male.

"What the...?"

That was all Mason got out before a fist slammed into his jaw. He stumbled back a few steps, dragging Gina with him, then took a vicious blow to the midsection that sent him to his knees.

Still, he wouldn't release Gina's wrist. But instead of fighting and twisting, she was now on her knees beside him and waving her free hand frantically.

"Dev! Stop!"

Sarah was terrified her sister might be hurt in the melee. Or the baby. Dear God, the baby. She leaped forward and hung like a monkey from Dev's arm.

"For God's sake, be careful! She's pregnant!"

The frantic shout backed Dev off but produced the opposite reaction in Mason. His brown eyes blazing, he wrenched Gina around to face him.

"Pregnant? What the hell is this? When you called me last night, all weepy and hysterical, you said you'd just come back from the clinic."

"I *had* just come back from the clinic!"

"Then what…?" His glance shot to her stomach, ripped back to her face. "You didn't do it?"

"I…I couldn't."

"But you couldn't be bothered to mention that little fact before I walked out on a critical floor vote, jumped a plane and flew all night to help you through a crisis you *also* didn't bother to tell me about until last night."

"So I didn't choose my words well," Gina threw back. "I was upset."

"Upset? You were damned near incoherent."

"And you were your usual arrogant self. Let me go, dammit."

She wrenched her wrist free and scrambled to her feet. Mason followed her up, his angry glance going from her to their small but intensely interested audience. His eyes narrowed on Sarah.

"You must be the sister."

"I… Yes."

His jaw working, he shifted to Dev. "Who the hell are you?"

"The sister's fiancé."

"What!" Gina's shriek ricocheted off the walls. "Since when?"

"It's a long story," Sarah said weakly. "Why don't we, uh, go someplace a little more private and I'll explain."

"Let's go." Gina hooked an arm through Sarah's, then whirled to glare at the two men. "Not you. Not either of you. This is between me and my sister."

It wasn't, but Dev yielded ground. Mason was forced to follow suit, although he had to vent his feelings first.

"You, Eugenia Amalia Therése St. Sebastian, are the most irresponsible, irritating, thickheaded female I've ever met."

Her nostrils flaring, Gina tilted her chin in a way that would have made the duchess proud. "Then aren't you fortunate, Ambassador, that I refused to marry you."

* * *

Her regal hauteur carried her as far as the stairwell. Abandoning it on the first step, she yanked on Sarah's arm to hurry her up to their room. Once inside, she let the door slam and thrust her sister toward the sofa wedged into the turret sitting room.

"Sit." She pointed a stern finger. "Talk. Now."

Sarah sat, but talking didn't come easy. "It's a little difficult to explain."

"No, it's not. Start at the beginning. When and where did you meet Dev?"

"In New York. At my office. When he came to show me the surveillance video of you lifting his Byzantine medallion."

Gina's jaw sagged. "What Byzantine...? Oh! Wait! Do you mean that little gold-and-blue thingy?"

"That little gold-and-blue thingy is worth more than a hundred thousand pounds."

"You're kidding!"

"I wish I was. What did you do with it, Gina?"

"I didn't do anything with it."

"Dev's surveillance video shows the medallion sitting on its stand when you sashay up to the display shelves. When you sashay away, the medallion's gone."

"Good grief, Sarah, you don't think I stole it, do you?"

"No, and that's what I told him from day one."

"*He* thinks I stole it?"

The fury that flashed in her eyes didn't bode well for Devon Hunter.

"It doesn't matter what he thinks," Sarah lied. "What matters is that the medallion's missing. Think, sweetie, think. Did you lift it off its stand? Or knock it off by accident, so it fell behind the shelves, maybe?"

"I did lift it, but I just wanted to feel the surface. You know, rub a thumb over that deep blue enamel." Her forehead creased in concentration. "Then I heard someone coming and… Oh, damn! I must have slipped it into my pocket. It's probably still there."

"Gina!" The two syllables came out on a screech. "How could you not remember slipping a twelfth-century Byzantine medallion in your pocket?"

"Hey, I didn't know it was a twelfth-century *anything*. And I'd just taken the pregnancy test that morning, okay? I was a little rattled. I'm surprised I made it to work that evening, much less managed to smile and orchestrate Hunter's damned dinner."

She whirled and headed for the door. Sarah jumped up to follow.

"I'm going to rip him a new one," Gina fumed. "How *dare* he accuse me of…" She yanked open the door and instantly switched pronouns. "How *dare* you accuse me of stealing?"

The two men in the hall returned distinctly different frowns. Jack Mason's was quick and confused. Dev's was slower and more puzzled.

"You didn't take it?"

"No, Mr. High-and-Mighty Hunter, I didn't."

"Take what?" Mason wanted to know.

"Then where is it?"

"I'm guessing it's in the pocket of the jacket I wore that evening."

"So you *did* take it?"

"Take what?"

Sarah cut in. "Gina was just running a hand over the surface when she heard footsteps. She didn't want to be caught fingering it, so she slipped it into her pocket."

"Dammit!" the ambassador exploded. "What the hell are you three talking about it?"

"Nothing that concerns you," Gina returned icily. "Why are you in my room, anyway? I have nothing more to say to you."

"Tough. I've still got plenty to say to you."

Sarah had had enough. A night of gut-wrenching worry, little sleep, no breakfast and now all this shouting was giving her a world-class headache. Before she could tell everyone to please shut up, Dev hooked her elbow and edged her out the door. With his other hand, he pushed Mason inside.

"You take care of your woman. I'll take care of mine."

"Wait a minute!" Thoroughly frustrated, Gina stamped a foot. "I still don't know how or when or why you two got engaged. You can't just…"

Dev closed the door in her face.

"Ooh," Sarah breathed. "She'll make you pay for that."

He braced both hands against the wall, caging her in. "Do I look worried?"

What he looked was unshaven, red-eyed and pissed.

"What are you doing here?" she asked a little breathlessly. "When I called the Hôtel Verneuil a while ago, they told me you had some kind of crisis in your business and had to fly home."

"I had a crisis, all right, but it was here. We need to get something straight, Lady Sarah. From now on, it's not *my* sister or *your* business. We're in this together. Forever. Or at least until we deliver on that promise to give kid number four a cruise on the Seine."

Sixteen

The prewedding dinner was held on the evening of May 3 at Avery's, where Dev had first "proposed" to Sarah. He reserved the entire restaurant for the event. The wedding ceremony and reception took place at the Plaza the following evening.

Gina, who'd emerged from a private session with the duchess white-faced and shaking, had regained both her composure and some of her effervescence. She then proceeded to astonish both her sister and her grandmother by taking charge of the dinner, the wedding ceremony and the reception.

To pull them off, she'd enlisted the assistance of Andrew at the Plaza, who'd aged with immense dignity since that long-ago day he'd discreetly taken care of an inebriated presidential aide during Grandmama's soirée for the Sultan of Oman. Gina also formed a close alliance with Patrick Donovan, Dev's incredibly capable and supremely confident executive assistant.

All Sarah had to do was draw up her guest list and select her dress. She kept the list small. She wanted to *enjoy* her wedding, not feel as though she was participating in a carefully scripted media event. Besides, she didn't have any family other than Grandmama, Gina and Maria.

She did invite a number of close friends and coworkers—including Alexis. *Beguile*'s executive editor had admitted the Paris thing was a mistake of epic proportions, but swore she'd never intended to publish a single photo without Sarah's permission. As a peace offering/wedding present, she'd had the photos printed and inserted into a beautifully inscribed, gilt-edged scrapbook. Just to be safe, Sarah had also had her hand over the disk with the complete set of JPEGs.

Dev's guest list was considerably longer than his bride's. His parents, sisters, their spouses and various offspring had flown to New York four days before the wedding. Dev had arranged a whirlwind trip to New Mexico so Sarah could meet most of them. She'd gotten to know them better while playing Big Apple tour guide. She'd also gained more insight into her complex, fascinating, handsome fiancé as more of his friends and associates arrived, some from his Air Force days, some from the years afterward.

Elise and Jean-Jacques Girault had flown in from Paris the afternoon before the wedding, just in time for dinner at the Avery. Sarah wasn't surprised that Elise and Alexis formed an instant bond, but the sight of Madame Girault snuggled against one of Dev's friends during predinner cocktails made her a tad nervous.

"Uh-oh," she murmured to Dev. "Do you think she's trying to seduce him?"

"Probably."

She searched the crowded restaurant, spotted Monsieur Girault happily chatting with Gina and relaxed.

Her wedding day dawned sunny and bright. Gina once again assumed charge. She'd accepted Dev's offer of payment without a qualm and arranged a full day at a spa for the women in the wedding party. She, Sarah, the duchess,

Maria, Dev's mother and sisters and the two little nieces who would serve as flower girls all got the works. The adults indulged in massages, facials, manicures, pedicures and hair treatments. The giggling little girls had their hair done and their fingernails and toenails painted pale lavender.

Sarah had enjoyed every moment of it, but especially treasured the half hour lying next to her sister on side-by-side massage tables while their facial masks cleaned and tightened their pores. According to the attendant, the masks were made of New Zealand Manuka honey, lavender oils and shea butter, with the additive of bee venom, which reputedly gave Kate Middleton her glowing complexion.

"At fifty-five thousand dollars per bottle, the venom better produce results," Gina muttered.

Only the fact that their masks contained a single drop of venom each, thus reducing the treatment price to just a little over a hundred dollars, kept Sarah from having a heart attack. Reaching across the space between the tables, she took Gina's hand.

"Thanks for doing all this."

"You're welcome." Her sister's mouth turned up in one of her irrepressible grins. "It's easy to throw great parties when you're spending someone else's money."

"You're good at it."

"Yes," she said smugly, "I am."

Her grin slowly faded and her fingers tightened around Sarah's.

"It's one of the few things I *am* good at. I'm going to get serious about it, Sarah. I intend to learn everything I can about the event-planning business before the baby's born. That way, I can support us both."

"What about Jack Mason? How does he figure in this plan?"

"He doesn't."

"It's his child, too, Gina."

"He'll have as much involvement in the baby's life as he wants," she said stubbornly, "but not mine. It's time—past time—I took responsibility for myself."

Sarah couldn't argue with that, but she had to suppress a few doubts as she squeezed Gina's hand. "You know I'll help you any way I can. Dev, too."

"I know, but I've got to do this on my own. And you're going to have your hands full figuring how to meld your life with his. Have you decided yet where you're going to live?"

"In L.A., if we can convince Grandmama to move out there with us. Maria, too."

"They'll hate leaving New York."

"I know."

Sarah's joy in her special day dimmed. She'd had several conversations with the duchess about a possible move. None of them had ended satisfactorily. As an alternative, Dev had offered to temporarily move his base of operations to New York and commute to L.A.

"I just can't bear to think of Grandmama alone in that huge apartment."

"Well…" Gina hesitated, indecision written all over her face. "I know I just made a big speech about standing on my own two feet, but I hate the thought of her being alone, too. I could…I could move in with her until I land a job. Or maybe until the baby's born. If she'll have me, that is, which isn't a sure thing after the scathing lecture she delivered when I got back from Switzerland."

"Oh, Gina, she'll have you! You know she will. She loves you." Sarah's eyes misted. "Almost as much as I do."

"Stop," Gina pleaded, her own tears spouting. "You can't walk down the aisle with your eyes all swollen and red. Dev'll strangle me."

As Dev took his place under the arch of gauzy netting lit by a thousand tiny, sparkling lights, strangling his soon-to-be sister-in-law was the furthest thing from his mind.

He was as surprised as Sarah and the duchess at the way Gina had pulled everything together. So when the maid of honor followed two giggling flower girls down the aisle, he gave Gina a warm smile.

She returned it, but Dev could tell the sight of the unexpected, uninvited guest at the back of the room had shaken her. Mason stood with his arms folded and an expression on his face that suggested he didn't intend to return to Washington until he'd sorted some things out with the mother of his child.

Then the music swelled and Dev's gaze locked on the two women coming down the aisle arm in arm. Sarah matched her step to that of the duchess, who'd stated bluntly she did *not* require a cane to walk a few yards and give her granddaughter away. Spine straight, chin high, eyes glowing with pride, she did just that.

"I hope you understand what a gift I'm giving you, Devon."

"Yes, ma'am, I do."

With a small harrumph, the duchess kissed her granddaughter's cheek and took her seat. Then Sarah turned to Dev, and he felt himself fall into her smile. She was so luminous, so elegant. So gut-wrenchingly beautiful.

He still couldn't claim to know anything about haute couture, but she'd told him she would be wearing a Dior gown her grandmother had bought in Paris in the '60s. The body-clinging sheath of cream-colored satin gave Dev a whole new appreciation of what Sarah termed vintage. The neckline fell in a soft drape and was caught at each shoulder by a clasp adorned with soft, floating feathers. The same downy feathers circled her tiny pillbox cap with its short veil.

Taking the hand she held out to him, he tucked it close to his heart and grinned down at her.

"Are you ready for phase three, Lady Sarah?"

"I am," she laughed. "So very, very ready."

Epilogue

I must admit I approve of Sarah's choice of husband. I should, since I decided Devon Hunter was right for her even before he blackmailed her into posing as his fiancée. How absurd that they still think I don't know about the deception.

Almost as absurd as Eugenia's stubborn refusal to marry the father of her child. I would respect her decision except, to borrow the Bard's immortal words, the lady doth protest too much. I do so dislike the sordid, steaming cauldron of modern politics, but I shall have to learn more about this Jack Mason. In the meantime, I'll have the inestimable joy of watching Eugenia mature into motherhood—hopefully!

From the diary of Charlotte,
Grand Duchess of Karlenburgh

* * * * *

Wrap up warm this winter with Sarah Morgan…

Sleigh Bells in the Snow

Kayla Green loves business and hates Christmas.

So when Jackson O'Neil invites her to Snow Crystal Resort to discuss their business proposal… the last thing she's expecting is to stay for Christmas dinner. As the snowflakes continue to fall, will the woman who doesn't believe in the magic of Christmas finally fall under its spell…?

4th October

www.millsandboon.co.uk/sarahmorgan

1013/MB435

She's loved and lost — will she ever learn to open her heart again?

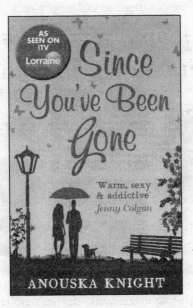

From the winner of ITV Lorraine's Racy Reads, Anouska Knight, comes a heart-warming tale of love, loss and confectionery.

'The perfect summer read — warm, sexy and addictive!'
—Jenny Colgan

For exclusive content visit:
www.millsandboon.co.uk/anouskaknight

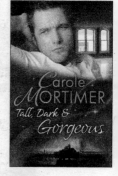

Join the Mills & Boon Book Club

Subscribe to **Desire**™ today for
3, 6 or 12 months and you could
save over £30!

We'll also treat you to these fabulous extras:

- 🌹 FREE L'Occitane gift set
  worth £10

- 🌹 FREE home delivery

- 🌹 Rewards scheme, exclusive
  offers…and much more!

Subscribe now and save over £30
www.millsandboon.co.uk/subscribeme

SUBS/OFFER/D1

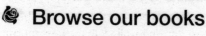